GOOD
GIRLS
BLUSH

Diane DePhillips

authorHOUSE®

AuthorHouse™
1663 Liberty Drive
Bloomington, IN 47403
www.authorhouse.com
Phone: 1-800-839-8640

Published by AuthorHouse   03/23/2015

ISBN: 978-1-4969-6174-7 (sc)
ISBN: 978-1-4969-6172-3 (hc)
ISBN: 978-1-4969-6173-0 (e)

Library of Congress Control Number: 2014922823

DEDICATIONS

To my parents, Michael and Theresa Bell
DePhillips, for a loving childhood

and

To Linda Stober, Lisa Redington and Chris Ranallo

CHAPTER 1

I arrive home to lavender lilacs tied with a pink satin cord at my front door. Mixed with the glorious fragrance is a man's cologne -- but, which scent, *Polo* or *Safari?*

In other words, *who* left the hothouse bundle -- Frankie, sporting *Polo,* or Clancy, donning *Safari?*

My name is Maria Magliani. I'm a forty-something bottle-blond saucy-entrepreneur, hell-bent on success and satisfaction -- Jagger style. Daddy always boasts that I acquired poise and self-confidence in

college. I also mastered the art of manipulation --
the procedure performed *without* a chiropractor.

Previously my former flame, Frankie Pirelli and
new heartthrob Clancy McClavey joined forces in
seeking my affections. Shamefully I admit to toying
with their egos. Frankie, a high school sweetheart,
hails from a prominent Sicilian family, anchored in
waste management. Clancy, by contrast, descends
from Irish blood lines and proudly holds the title,
Fire Marshal for the City of Des Moines.

I pick up the purple flowers, and after sensing hot
breath on my neck, I pivot and smile. "Oh, it's you.
I might have known."

Poised before me stands wild child Frankie,
peering with intensity and reeking of *Polo* cologne.
He beams too with an apparent visual stimulation,
rekindling a fire in me. He lifts the house key from
my hand and slides it into the lock. He shoves the
door open and hustles me inside. Pinning me against
one of the etched-glass side-lights, he hunkers down
and begins his pursuit by planting smooches on my
cheeks, then all over my face, ears, arms...parts
palpitate while passions rage. What's a girl to do?

* * *

I debated my options; though, after a flash of
apprehension, I rammed full-steam into a flesh-to-
flesh tango with Frankie, eventually culminating in

2

a three-month tryst. Once the emotional ride was over, I found myself "Alone Again (Naturally)."

My cell rings, snarling my daydream.

"Hey, Maria," a husky voice charges the air.

"'What's up, Clancy?" I blink as I'm welcomed back to reality.

"Just finished a twenty-four-hour shift," he announces. "I was thinking after a quick nap, we might cruise to Ranaldo's on 3rd for Baked Cavatelli and Steak de Burgo. I love the way Chef Pietro prepares the sauce for the beef."

"Perfect." I salivate, rubbing my hands with pleasure. "Oh yeah, the sauce: garlic, basil, butter. Scrumptious. What time you thinkin'?"

"Around 7:00? I'll phone for reservations. Shouldn't be a problem on a Tuesday night."

I picture Clancy's powerful 6'2" build, with a swath of brown wavy hair framing emerald eyes. I could drown in those eyes. What in the world was I thinking when I succumbed to Frankie's advances? Point taken; I wasn't thinking. At least not with my head.

"Excellent. Want to rendezvous at my place or the restaurant?" His firm lips tinge my thoughts. Particularly the little void above the middle of his mouth. I imagine lashing my tongue over the impression, succeeded by the sparks from his tongue on my skin.

"I'll swing by and pick you up, Maria. That way I won't worry about you getting home later."

Wow. What a nice guy. Sounds romantic and reassuring. One person in this world is worried about me. A short time ago my husband, Michael died suddenly and mysteriously, leaving me to fend for our son, Chip, and two thriving restaurants. After my pizza pub unexpectedly roasted to the ground, and Chip was diagnosed with bipolar disorder, new-found friend, Clancy stepped up and bolstered me with emotional support.

"Sweet." I approve. "Come by after you catch some shuteye."

I click off. The dinner arrangements whet my appetite, though not as much as Clancy's bod. I smack my lips, then push away from the kitchen castle grey granite countertop, eager to design a polished sexy look for the firefighter.

I'll team a white silk sleeveless camisole with a geometric-print pencil skirt. Bare legs and patent pumps. At my neckline, dangling from silver chains will swing a small gemstone cross, a memento of my Catholic upbringing and a cue to remain in the state of grace.

I'll top off the outfit with a cropped, black chiffon bolero. After all, I am a black widow, poised to eat my prey.

Lord, I have been alone too long.

CHAPTER 2

Longing to escape the monotony of the day, I decompress by soaking in moisturizing bath beads -- *Calgon take me away* -- while key lime wafts from six soy votive candles canvassing the tub. Of late, I sold Tony's Deli so I can devote more time to my new avocation -- investing in real estate. In doing so, I surrender the camaraderie of employees from the restaurant industry, for more freedom and a less frazzled schedule.

I contact my financier at River Grove Bank to arrange a line of credit. Next I amass my team -- an electrician, plumber, painter, tile man, cooling and heating guy, and a carpenter. What's wrong with surrounding oneself with strapping, young men? As my grandmother, Nonnie says: "Look, but don't touch!" I can do all the gawking and drooling I want, just keep my hands to myself.

My first purchase four months ago was a fifty-year-old 1240 square-foot two-story apartment-turned-townhome on Sherry Lane. After minor fixes and fresh paint, I was lucky to lease it with a year contract. My current venture is a 988 square-foot bungalow, built in 1925, located in the Cedar Ridge district, near inner city and in desperate need of restoration. I enjoy the grunt work but my body takes a toll. Presumably the swirling tub will aid me in submerging my aches and pain.

My cell sings. I recognize cousin, Rocco Randazzo's number from the Des Moines Detective's Bureau.

"Hey, buddy, what's good?" I ask, fumbling to draw down the whirlpool jets.

"Maria, curious if you've been following the story out east about Catholic priests molesting altar boys?"

"Yeah, saw a segment on CNN a couple of nights ago. As I recall, two priests and a lay teacher passed around a fourteen-year-old lad for sexual gratification. Sick. My dad would have skinned those perverts alive if they had ever touched my brother Nick, when we attended St. Monica's. Of course in our day, you only heard about dirty tricks with little *girls*. Life certainly has changed."

"Jesus, Maria, you are so fucking naïve." Rocco sasses. "Depraved behavior has been around as long as man, and it favors no gender. Trust me; boys are just as vulnerable as girls. I sometimes forget how shielded you were growing up -- in a bubble."

"Okay, smartass, where are you going with this?" I shake my head after his verbal lashing, though he might be right about the sheltered shot. Then again, I might have embraced ignorance while coming of age in my large, loving Italian family. "In our day, daughters labored over women's work -- cooking, cleaning, and caretaking; sons mowed lawns, shoveled snow, and played sports. Curfew at midnight or you'd turn into a pumpkin."

"Pump the brakes on childhood memories, Maria and gnaw on this: for the past three months I've been involved with a federal multi-jurisdictional task force investigating a string of drug-related sexual assaults. Kind of a mouthful, but you catch my drift."

"Ten-four," I assure him, twisting toward the spa faucets to add more hot water. "Tell me, Rocco, what's the delivery method, and are the altar boys the targets?"

"You're ahead of me, girl. We seized a cache of liquid GHB, the date-rape drug in Iowa City. In addition, we've confiscated a large quantity in Ames and Des Moines. We believe scofflaws used the illegal compound to bait juveniles by spiking their drinks -- Kool-Aid, Diet Coke, alcohol. The drugs are eliminated from the digestive system in four to sixteen hours, which makes the crime difficult to constrain."

"Disgusting." I blurt. "So, innocent kids drank Communion wine combined with narcotics while serving Mass?"

"Possibly. Youngsters were coaxed to imbibe at church, school outings, and overnight youth camps," Rocco confesses. "Any enticement necessary for pedophiles and addicts to get what they want. Greedy bastards."

"Though with those drugs, wouldn't you detect a smell or taste?" My lips tighten, I shake my head and shudder from the sheer offensiveness.

"No way," Rocco argues. "This stuff is odorless and invisible. It has a slight saltiness on its own, yet it dissolves instantly in soda, juice, liquor or beer, with no residue."

"I imagine GHB is classified as a predatory drug. I've read that along with leaving its victims incapable of resisting sexual advances, they can't remember much either." I narrow my eyes, speculating on my usefulness to Rocco.

"Maria, I want to include you in our sting," he proposes. "Admittedly, we're just now formulating our plan, but I'm confident in your contacts and capabilities. Are you up for the challenge?"

I hesitate, pondering why Rocco and the Des Moines Police Department would invite *me* into their secret maneuvers. Gnashing my teeth, I straighten my back and anticipate my dance with danger.

"I'm in."

CHAPTER 3

Clancy texts that he's on his way.

Struggling with dating after my life-long marriage to Michael, I reflect on my wedding day-- white lace, cello and violins, champagne. Pictures of a couple, a girl with anxious eyes, a boy with a crooked grin, locked in love. For better, for worse, we vowed. Even when hips spread and skin stretched, I would be loved for a lifetime. But, whose lifetime, as I sit at the kitchen table, alone.

* * *

I recharge when the doorbell chimes.

I scuttle to the entry, peek through slats of the wood blinds covering one of the latticed windows, to take in the full view of Clancy. My gaze rests on his impressive eyes and expansive chest. Well, maybe not in that order.

My hand trembles a bit as I twist the knob.

"Maria, you look ridiculously hot," he praises, taking my hand and twirling me around.

"Ditto, Chief. Nice threads." Debonair Clancy is decked out in navy dress slacks, a white oxford shirt, and a blue and white seersucker blazer. Instantly I know I want to jump him.

He leans in and softly pecks me on the neck. Then he backs off, flashes a smile and resumes again, first tenderly, then more urgently.

"Whoa, buddy, slow down. We have the whole night ahead and besides, Chip's inside." I admire his spunky charm, but there's a time and place for hanky-panky. All the while my pate swirls a bit from the aroma of his spicy after-shave.

My son, now a seventeen-year-old senior at Immaculate Mary, saddled with university brochures from Iowa, Arizona State and my alma mater, Drake, is striving to complete registration forms on his laptop.

"Yes, ma'am," hails Clancy, as he clicks his heels and salutes. "I'm sorry, Maria, you fricking turn me on. I want to slide my hand up under your dress and ...”

"Do naughty things? Sorry, Charlie," I murmur in hushed tones, jostling to untangle from Clancy. Nevertheless, I'm aware that good girls have catching up to do; as a result, we are drawn to bad boys. Remaining to be seen: What constitutes a bad boy? And conversely: Are good girls always good?

"Let me tell Chip I'm leaving. We'll meet up at the driveway." Clancy's keen eyes roll back as he saunters toward his car, a classic '66 robin-egg blue Jaguar XKE.

CHAPTER 4

My thoughts channel back to Chip, who discovered soccer at eight-years-old as his father and I struggled to harness his energy. His neighborhood chum, Andrew suggested the two join a rec team. Surprisingly the team trainer recognized both boys' speed and agility and recommended they escalate to a competitive league.

Little did we know how much our lives would be impacted with the affiliation. Endless hours of practice, delayed dinners, weekend travel, and interrupted holidays left us, as parents, frazzled on occasion. Years of numb fingers and toes, a scorched throat, aching ears from the cold, left Chip more dedicated than ever. Now our son is being recruited by a Division 1 school, which could materialize into thousands of dollars saved in tuition.

* * *

"Hey, Mom, got a call from the coach at Old Dominion University today," beams Chip. "He's aware that I set the school record for the most goals -- 22. Wants me to come and play at ODU this fall."

"Awesome. That's the Colonial Athletic Conference, isn't it?"

"You bet. Coach is sending me a ticket to Norfolk for a campus tour," he affirms with boyish enthusiasm. "He thinks I might be eligible for an academic scholarship too. He admitted they love kids from the Midwest – athletic, and smart as well."

"Nice recruiting tool -- Virginia Beach." Promptly my mind flies to KAYAK and airline connections between Norfolk and Des Moines. I also imagine long weekends with me prone on the sand absorbing the sun and Janet Evanovich's *Stephanie Plum Novels* on Kindle. "Did you register with the National Student Clearinghouse for release of your transcripts to the NCAA?"

"Got it covered, Mom. Hey, remember what Dad used to say, 'the harder you work, the luckier you get?' This could be my chance to prove him right."

Chip is totally jazzed. Rightfully so. Even now he's inspired by his father. I reach over and tousle his hair with my hand.

"You'll give it your best, honey. I know you will."

"Thanks, Mom. Now, get out of here," he orders.

I snag my handbag and phone, detecting a red flashing light announcing a missed message from Rocco: *"Maria, our investigation has morphed to include a sixteen-year-old girl's disappearance."*

"Gimme a call."

CHAPTER 5

I text Rocco that I will phone him in the morning. Don't want to start off on the wrong foot -- dissing his call.

He replies: *"No worries. Touch base in the a.m."*

I tap in the garage code, the doors roll down and I strut toward Clancy and his ride. He leaps out of the driver's seat and escorts me to the passenger side. I blush at the gleam in his eye and the snicker on his face. What in God's name am I in for?

"Hey, babe," he smirks, "wanna spin by my house for a cocktail or aperitif before dinner?"

I mentally drool at the prospect; after which the devil on my shoulder jousts his pitchfork, lancing my resolve. Certainly by hanging at Clancy's, I place myself in the near occasion of sin. A Catholic no-no. I consider, is that like a *near miss* in aviation? As I fiddle with the crystal cross that brushes my chest, I acknowledge I am a dull dog indeed.

"You know, I'm good." I protest. "How 'bout first we indulge at Ranaldo's, then figure out later, *later?*" Smooth, I think.

"Agreed. "But, don't think you're getting off that easy, Maria."

What does he mean by *"getting off"?* Is he speaking literally or figuratively?

"Hey, Mars Man, have you read *Men Are from Mars, Women Are from Venu*s, the ultimate guide clarifying the differences between the sexes? Do guys ever *not* speak in sexual innuendos?" Unconsciously, I tug closed my bolero to prevent aroused nipples from piercing through my sheer cami.

"No, and no. I haven't read your trashy novel. And we pretty much speak about sex, dream about sex, and have sex, both literally and figuratively, all the time. We relate everything to sex. Ain't life grand?" he brags.

I contemplate the adage: *Men think about sex every seven seconds,* or on the low end, nineteen times a day.

"Riveting." I muse. "My mind is looping Lady Antebellum's Grammy winner, 'Need You Now.' When a woman is alone, she needs a man. When a man is drunk, he needs a woman. Did I get that right?"

Why in the hell am I so defensive? This probably has little to do with Clancy. Our repartee continues with the sexual tension elevating until we reach the restaurant in Ankeny, a suburb of Des Moines. At that point, my date parks the Jag, unbuckles himself, then embraces me with a long, wet deep kiss. His tongue traces over my lips, alerting body parts in us both. I sit pulsing to his touch.

"I'm sorry, Maria, what was the question?" he poses with a blank expression. "You ask a lot of questions."

I wriggle free from the car restraint.

"No biggie. Let's eat."

CHAPTER 6

When we gather in the bistro lobby, I'm particularly impressed by the subdued ambience and beautiful appointments of warm woods and low lighting. Our waitress, Tosha requests drink orders, recommending Freixenet, distinguished California champagne. The wine exhibits a crisp texture with a hint of ginger and pepper at the finish. We are definitely onboard with the bubbly.

The menu displays an Italian-American fare. We elect the much-heralded Steak de Burgo, a deux. In addition we share a chopped salad slathered with homemade Creamy Parmesan Dressing, bottled and sold on the premises. We choose asparagus for the veggie, but skip the starches for the piece de resistance, Crème Brulee -- rich custard, served cold, torched with a burnt caramel layer atop.

* * *

Clancy and I are sipping decaf coffee when his white cloth napkin floats to the floor. He curls down, grasping it, along with my leg.

"Oh!" I flinch, as quivers run further north. "You caught me off guard."

"Lucky me, huh? Maria, what a fabulous dinner, only surpassed by the company. What say we head back to my place for a Bailey's Irish Cream or a crème de menthe? Really warms the innards."

"Thanks, I enjoyed the meal too." I speculate about Clancy's *warming* practice before glancing at my Movado watch: 9:02 p.m. "Sure, your place is a possibility," I answer -- less than enthusiastic, realizing my virtue may be at risk. I figure I can always scrub his after-dinner cordial suggestion later.

Pietro, the culinary artiste, donning a pressed white double-breasted chef coat, moseys over to our table on his rotation of the restaurant. Clancy commends him and promises to write an online review at *tripadvisor.com,* scoring five stars for "Elegant dining in an atmosphere of distinction."

My cell vibrates, I peek down and recognize Chip's number. A tad tipsy, I excuse myself, cross the room, heading toward the arrow marked *Ladies.* A chill of fear shivers down my spine because I didn't expect to hear from my son.

After punching *TALK* I hear: *"Mom, my friend Lily is missing."*

CHAPTER 7

Lily Timmons, a junior at Immaculate Mary, stands 5'6", 110 pounds, with a heart-shaped face, scalloped-edged with silken strands of black beauty, the product of an English-Latin gene pool. Infused with a parochial background, and a lack of nooky knowledge, she is much sought after by guys competing for her V-card.

Her soul mate, Tyler Stroud, a lanky eighteen-year-old college freshman at Iowa State, with a square jaw and lively eyes, parades Lily proudly at his fraternity house.

"Hey, man, what's with the chick?" babbles an upperclassman. After eyeing her up and down, he prattles, "Hello, sweetheart. Sorry man, no outsiders are allowed when the chapter meeting convenes. I swear you pledges are all morons."

"Oh yeah, I know," Tyler squints and shrugs. "She just came by to see my crib."

"Bro, love where your head's at, but wouldn't call it your crib quite yet. You have to lock in a *C* average for semester grades, pass all your final exams, and survive initiation, before you score your own man cave."

Prevailing wisdom should have warned Lily about socializing with college men. But Tyler, a companion from Catholic Youth Camp, respects her chaste, innocent nature and even crows about it. Unquestionably she is not a girl with her feet in the street.

Her boyfriend rarely participates in the rowdy all-night raves hosted at Memorial Union, and he repeatedly snubs euphoric stimulants like Ecstasy, which are readily available on campus.

Lily and her beau, squirrel away into the first empty room available, praying for enough private time to caress and cuddle before the Alpha Phi Epsilon assembly. Tyler's dorm mate, Brady is also touring the frat house.

"Hey partner, how's about you give me and Lily a few minutes to ourselves?" he urges.

Brady -- a short, affable, red-headed pledge brother -- and his roomie both love rap, Jameson Whiskey and supermodels. Especially supermodels.

"Sure dude, knock yourself out. Better make it a quickie though. The weekly powwow is set to start in the Gathering Room in five."

"Lily, I need to join the others. Take the Wrangler and I'll text you when I'm through," he reassures her. "We can kick it then."

He bends down and she graces him with a soft moist kiss on his parted lips. His heart throbs as he reluctantly releases her intertwined arms.

Lily waves her hand and lip-synchs *Bye-bye*. As she weaves through the room to exit, her gaze is drawn toward the center, to a tall, brawny, handsome guest speaker, garbed in drapes of brown broadcloth. Braided rope is fastened around his waist and a cork crucifix hangs from his neck. His haunting eyes *creep* her out.

CHAPTER 8

"Gentlemen, my name is Father Paul Vincensi. You can call me Paul, Father, whatever. I want to bring you and your God closer together with a new application for your iPad or iPhone. The $1.99 'Confession: The Roman Catholic App aims to assist you in your examination of conscience -- recalling your sins, one Commandment at a time."

Eyes fly open wide as Father Paul proceeds to expound on the declining frequency of Americans who receive the penitential sacrament. Kevin, the local Greek president, springs up and darts to the center to join him.

"Father, why don't we open a dialogue here. Questions and comments?"

Arguably the group is stunned by the priest's presentation, although a handful of attendees feign interest. Father Paul clarifies that religious apps are not new. Inspirational daily text messages have been available since mobile technology expanded, often frequented by Muslims on their road to Mecca.

"Father, if I track my offenses online, will I be forgiven?" Tyler inquires, conceivably guilty of petting or *noodling* -- the art of fishing with one's hands.

"No, son, this process helps you prepare for Confession. You will still need to visit and receive absolution from a flesh-and-blood priest. The app also contains a written 'Act of Contrition' which would be recited by the sinner, followed by, *Amen.*"

Another frat brother shifts in his seat before broaching a controversial subject among advocates: "Is it true Father, it's a sin to use artificial contraception -- like *the pill* -- even in marriage?"

"Yes, at this time the only acceptable birth control allowed among Roman Catholics is abstinence."

The guys glare at each other gasping in disbelief. A few laugh out loud.

"Seriously, you must be fucking kidding," bellows the Chapter Master. "Pardon my mouth, Father. I know sex outside of marriage is a mortal sin, but didn't Pope Benny relax the policy for contraception?" Kevin shakes his head in annoyance.

"In truth, Pope Benedict XVI has reversed course on condom use -- to preserve life and avoid death in the spread of AIDS."

"Excellent;" someone shouts from the peanut gallery, "so, if you're gay or in Africa, you and your condom are good to go."

"Joking aside, gentlemen, it remains to be seen how our new Argentine leader, Pope Francis will reign. He's noted for having a compassionate spirit and a compromising nature, while also exhibiting a devotion to the church's traditional values and doctrines."

"Hey Father, what's the word on abortion?" a pledge asks. He's a typical underclassman -- young and dumb -- with a wooly beard and upturned nose. Perchance a brother or two has frantically scoured local pharmacies at 6:00 a.m. for morning-after pills or "Plan B," resulting from a night of unprotected sexual adventure.

"Men, the Catholic Church condemns all abortions for whatever reason," including RU486 -- medication abortion -- prescribed for rape and incest victims."

The guys are getting pissed off, so Father attempts to dial down the animosity. "Let's explore these avenues in our next get-together," he recommends.

Kevin thanks Father Paul and proceeds to new business at hand -- Tricks for Treats Party.

* * *

While Lily lounges in Tyler's Jeep in the fraternity parking lot, she phones her mom to update her whereabouts, and then starts texting girlfriend, Nataliya.

Her eyes flutter when she's stunned by a rap on the driver-side window.

CHAPTER 9

Meanwhile, Chip's bulletin -- his classmate Lily is missing -- trips my sober trigger. Tears splash down my face, even though I don't know her personally. I return from the Ladies Lounge to our table and alert Clancy.

"Sorry, I need to bail. Something's come up at home." Also, I feel obliged to contact Rocco regarding the turn of events, unsure if he is aware of the news.

"For sure. Let's head out."

I appreciate his reaction and his respect for my privacy. Once I'm secured in my seat, he eases in on his side, shucks the foiled leftovers into the rear compartment, twists his neck toward me, inches in closer and skims his lips over mine. Without hesitation he drives his tongue deep in my mouth, signaling a rush of heat throughout. Instinctively his arms fling out, foraging for breasts. Likewise, his kisser follows.

He snatches up my middle finger and plunks it in his yap, sucking like a newborn piglet. Nasty! Even though I am aware of the confined space of the sports car, and the positioning of the gear shift, The Raspberries' tune, "Please Go All the Way" looms to mind, heightening my exhilaration. Obviously that ain't gonna happen, yet at the same time Clancy, with boyish enthusiasm and persistence, takes matters into his own hands by unzipping his pants and...

My cell sings. Startled, I raise my eyebrows, particularly when I recognize the pre-set ringer identifying Rocco. Perfect timing. Clancy pauses briefly when I announce with a faint smile, "Babe, let's pick this up later."

I remember boys in school days pleading they would suffer blue balls if a girl didn't complete the task at hand. Really? Sounded kind of desperate. Even so, Clancy genuinely looks pained after my proposal to take a break. I wonder if he sees the hidden pity in my eyes. And again, I dread being referred to as frigid, a prick tease or prude...so I finish the job.

Rocco's voicemail records with an assigned sound.

"Okay, Maria, now you're off the hook." Then Clancy bargains, "You go tend to your business and I'll catch some *zzz*'s."

Of course he wants a siesta -- the man blazed through a twenty-four-hour shift fighting fires. After which, I may also have ignited some inner flames.

He drops me off at home and we agree to talk tomorrow, Wednesday. I let out a big breath. He *whooshes* away. Immediately I press #1, to play Rocco's voicemail message.

CHAPTER 10

"Maria, you may not be apprised of the disappearance of a teenage girl, Lily Timmons. In addition, new allegations have surfaced involving child pornography and the installation of a hidden video camera in the Immaculate Mary's boys' bathroom. Prosecutors have traced these acts to Chip's high school principal. Call me when you get this."

I plop down into a green and white striped canvas front porch swing, wasting no time returning his call.

"Rocco, for God's sake, is no one safe?" I groan.

"It's fucking nuts, Maria. First, a young girl disappears. Now, some douche bag sets out to capture boys using the restroom, then releases the images on the Internet. Despicable comes to mind."

"Do you figure a connection between this dirtball and Lily's disappearance?"

"All things are possible," Rocco confirms. "We want to talk to Chip, with your permission, and utilize him as our go-between. We've already collared the principal, David Sheldon."

My eyes slide into slits as concern consumes m, contemplating my son's participation in the scenario.

"Why would you engage Chip?"

"Maria, we need an insider in school. He's an outgoing kid, likeable, well situated with the student body. We believe Chip could attract trust from other students."

I grow more reluctant in using my kiddo as a pawn -- the hairs on my neck bristle. How close do I want him to brazen, sexual misconduct?

"I don't know, Rocco. Let me think about it and discuss it with him."

I end the call, my heart at odds with my head. I fret about placing my child in jeopardy -- even though the risk is probably small. I spread my hand over my face, squeeze my eyes shut and chant a prayer for guidance.

CHAPTER 11

After rapping on Lily's window, Father Paul Vincensi introduces himself in the parking lot of the fraternity.

"I'm sorry to bother you," he admonishes, "but my vehicle won't start. Hoped you might give me a hand with a boost from my jumper cables. It should only take a minute."

His big black eyes dart surreptitiously, surveying the area. The priest points to a 1989 scruffy tan Volkswagen utility van, adorned with yellow-and-white daisies and emblazoned in brown script *PEACE*

OUT on each side panel. The blue license plates display: CHURCH 2.

Lily abandons her cell and flashes her attention toward the rusted-out creased jalopy. No surprise in her mind the beast won't start -- it's a miracle it made it this far.

"The thing is," she remarks, "you should get somebody else. I'm not at all familiar with mechanical gizmos." She figures neither is this guy. Hasn't he ever seen MTV's "Pimp My Ride" or the BBC's "Top Gear," shows she's flipped through with boyfriend Tyler in his dorm room?

"That's cool," Father responds. "My battery's probably dead because A, I left the lights on, or B, the water in the battery evaporated." He scratches his head and grimaces. "Then again, it could be the alternator. Beyond that I don't know. But if you wouldn't mind me opening your hood, I could connect the positive and negative cables to the posts and try to get a charge. I really need to shove off; I have to officiate a funeral."

Come on, the dude is wrapped in robes and rocks a crucifix, she thinks. How dodgy can a man of the cloth be? She feels guilty denying his request. "Alright, whatever," she mumbles, disregarding her internal panic compass when the needle records: *PURE EVIL.*

"Terrific." Father Paul grins as he wrenches open her door. "Now scooch over and I'll pull up beside the van. That way I can attach the cables."

At once Lily is struck with a rush of dread. She turns to the priest and whispers, "Sorry I forgot something. I need to go now."

CHAPTER 12

Too late. He smothers her face with a white over-sized flax linen handkerchief drenched in chloroform. He confiscates her cell phone and ganks her small coral-colored Fossil bag from the passenger side floor of the Jeep. The priest jerks open the van's rear cargo access, plunging Lily on top of a blue vinyl air mattress.

Father Paul rockets toward the rectory, where he can be left uninterrupted with his conquest. He knows he only has a short time before the organic compound wears off -- somewhere between minutes and a few hours.

First, Lily's extremities will go numb; next, her vision and hearing will fail. At that point the substance causes a reaction by releasing gases that will render her unconscious.

He whirls into the parish garage and quickly closes it by punching the remote. After propping open the van's side hatch, he beholds his prize. He leaves the door ajar so the filtered light allows him to savor the sight and delight of Lily. He hoists her short, stone-washed jean skirt up to her waist, pulls off her pink lace trouser-cut panties and stuffs them under his waist sash. He separates her legs.

Swiping a hand over his slobbering mouth, he anticipates the contact. The priest cradles her lower limbs, lassoing her legs over his shoulders, after which he orally violates her. He starts ejaculating on himself prior to flipping her over and entering her backside. Jack-rabbit thrusts trim his gratification time, when he climaxes again. He defiles her vaginally; but then worries she will awaken soon, so he clumsily fashions her undies back on and adjusts her miniskirt.

"Mmmm," Lily moans, unable to identify the origin of the pain. Her fingers rest on her forehead which she rubs to alleviate the migraine. She attempts to swallow, but her throat stings and tastes of metal. Her eyes fail to focus and her bottom burns.

What in the hell has happened? She can't recall, but gawking in front of her is Father Paul.

"Lily, you were struck by a hit-and-run driver," insists the priest. He peers around, then grapples for another crippling agent for her to ingest-- one that will provide the same desired result.

"Here, drink this!" He shoves a Diet Coke in her face, laced with the diabolical designer-drug, GHB.

Lily tries to gather her senses, but a flush of confusion and nausea sweeps over her. When she tries to stand, her legs wobble like Jell-O.

"Okay, I'll take a few sips to help me feel right again." She complies.

* * *

That's the last thing Lily remembers.

CHAPTER 13

After Clancy wheels me home, I eyeball Chip when I reach the kitchen. He's on his phone chatting with girlfriend Nataliya about Lily's disappearance. He casts a glance my way, then disconnects.

"Mom, word has it that Lily's boyfriend, Tyler was the one who discovered she was missing. How brutal is that?" His shoulders slump in defeat. "Imagine if it had been Nataliya? I'd freak."

He leaps up, pacing repeatedly around the stone top center island, noticeably fighting back tears, shaken to the core.

"Chip, I'm sorry. It sucks. All of it -- Lily gone missing, the videotaping in the school bathroom, your principal's arrest."

I don't know if he's aware of the inappropriate actions of priests, so I don't include that element of chaos. I approach my son, embrace him, then clutch his hand, piloting him to the counter bar stools.

"Sit down dear; I want to run something by you." My back stiffens, I clasp my hands together and continue in a grave tone. "Rocco wants to engage you as an envoy or agent between the kids at school and the Des Moines Police Department."

Chip's eyes fly open wide. He cocks his head and wrinkles his brow. "For real? In what way?"

"The cops need an insider -- an intermediary. You are a go-to guy, Chip. People respect you; you foster trust. For Heaven's sake, you're the class president. Who knows, you may even draw out leads from staff and teachers. Rocco believes in you." I figure my cousin can give him a heads up on the GHB scandal when he deems it necessary.

Rattled, he crouches, biting his nails, looking intently. He speculates when he asks, "Does that make me an informant -- a rat, a snitch?"

"Of course not," I reassure him. "This isn't 'Law and Order', and you're not turning state's evidence against John Gotti. You'd be a liaison. You would pass on to the police anything that might benefit in the

CHAPTER 14

I encounter my first yawn of the evening. After peering up at the "Sticks" hand-painted birch wall clock -- 10:32 p.m., I savor one of the border captions: "Seize the Day, Relish the Night." I waste no time firing off emails to my sub-contractors to assemble in the morning. I text Chip's cell number to Rocco so they can connect.

I compile a basket of clean folded clothes from the laundry, before bolting to my room. My head no sooner hits the bed, when I stretch for a string of aquamarine-quartz rosary beads, nestled beneath my pillow. My deceased husband, Michael surprised me with them on our 5th wedding anniversary jaunt to New York. I'd spotted them at St. Patrick's Cathedral.

The Holy Rosary, a religious practice first initiated by eastern Christian monks in the third century, is a collection of meditative prayers, following the lives of Jesus and Mary from the Annunciation to the Ascension. It is Tuesday night so I will recite the Sorrowful Mysteries as most recently decreed by Pope John Paul 11 in 2002.

I rush through the Apostles' Creed, six Our Fathers, fifty-three Hail Mary's, six Glory Be's and the closing mantra -- Hail Holy Queen. Also included between each decade is the Blessed Virgin Mary's request from the children at Fatima:

"Oh my Jesus, forgive us our sins,
save us from the fires of hell,
lead all souls to Heaven,
especially those most in need of your Mercy."

I offer a special intention for Lily's safe return.

Weary but wakeful, I rewind a Sherlock Holmes audiotape, "The Problem of Thor Bridge," written by Arthur Conan Doyle, published in *The Strand Magazine* in 1929. In the tale, Holmes and Watson are employed by a gold-mining magnate to prove the innocence of his children's governess, accused of murdering his wife. Light reading before bed.

My phone rings -- Clancy.

"Hey babe, did you get squared away?"

My mind's eye computes the day's success rate and emphatically I resound, "More or less."

"I had a fabulous night," he reiterates. "Hope we can do it again soon. What's on the agenda for tomorrow? Wanna catch lunch? I'm thinkin' pizza slices."

"Ditto on the date, pizza sounds great," I remark.

After a short hesitation, Clancy's next question, "Maria, what are you wearing?"

After an awkward silence I reply, *"Nothing..."*

CHAPTER 15

Wednesday morning I arise like clockwork at 5:03 a.m., rested and ready to rule the world. I shuffle to the kitchen, reheat coffee that remains from yesterday, and measure the liquid for my wheat bread recipe. I dissolve packaged yeast in the java, add honey, salt, butter, fresh ground cinnamon, and a combination of white and whole wheat flour. After incorporating the ingredients, I knead the dough, place it in a covered bowl in the oven, setting the timer for an hour.

I brew a fresh cup of Starbuck's Sumatra, perch atop a counter barstool, then I log onto the Internet, eager to check email. Fortunately my subs respond that they can rendezvous at 10:00 a.m. Hopefully that allows me enough time to discuss business and also hook up with Clancy at noon -- okay, meet up with him in any case.

Before exiting the computer, I confirm my bank balance, pay bills, and order a hand-painted Lolita wine glass, bedecked with whimsical designs - blue, green, and lavender stones, glitter, and inscribed *#1 MOM.* The stemware is a birthday present for my mother Pauline, a sixty-five-year-old modern matriarch. She has been my inspiration for forty odd years -- smart, loyal, honest and kicky! Yeah, a lady that parades in four-inch stilettos every day definitely deserves -- *kicky.*

* * *

Elbows on the stone island, fists braced on my chin, I flashback to an image of me at three-years-old strolling a pink-gingham carriage on the sidewalk in front of our house. Inside the pram I haul my Mattel "Baby Tender Love" doll and unwittingly I also cart two grey bunnies huddled beneath flannel receiving blankets. I maneuver the carriage through a breezeway and a side entrance adjoining the mudroom of our home. Mother greets me, strips

58

away the covers and screams bloody murder when, instead of bunnies, she exposes two rats! She boots the stroller down the basement stairs, sealing off the pantry with a sliding pocket door, before hugging me incessantly. My hero.

Dad is summoned from work a few blocks away, where he owns and operates Francesco's Italian Restaurant, a bistro named after my grandfather. At the same time, brother Nick, my sister Jennie, and I are ushered to my parent's bedroom where we kneel with Mother to pray the rosary while Father slays the dragon -- well, prepares an ambush for the uninvited varmints. The sound of the *snap* of the traps continues to haunt me in early hours before stars surrender sparks.

Life was so simple then -- call Mom; call Dad.

CHAPTER 16

Fast-forward twenty years. I ruminate on my encounter with a gunman at our restaurant.

It was closing time, about midnight on a Friday evening, and I was assisting as hostess and cashier. Keen to meet up with boyfriend Michael after my shift, I focused on wrestling credit card receipts, tallying charges and counting cash.

Unawares, I shuddered when the front door slammed and an intruder barked, *"This is a stick up!"*

Terror struck when I perceived a tall, sinister, lean black teen brandishing a Saturday night special, trained at my head.

He proceeded to wield the cheap unreliable .25 caliber semi-automatic handgun, directing lingering patrons and employees behind the bar, face down on the floor. Revolting; considering we were practically licking leaky pop syrup, musty beer foam and splattered liqueurs from the dingy, sticky blue and white terrazzo.

He demanded that we surrender our jewelry, watches, cash and other valuables, after which we passed them up the line while he pocketed our dough. The assailant appeared to be high as a kite -- his speech rattled on like a repeater, his hands quivered, his face seeped sweat. He was clearly agitated. A plucky staff sous chef, startled, but stalwart, cleverly slinked away unnoticed to the kitchen, where he *dialed* -- yeah, an old concept -- the cops.

They arrived just as the thief scurried through the parking lot in an attempt to straddle his Schwinn. Unfortunately for the culprit, he was wounded when a policeman hollered, *"Stop or I'll shoot!"* and the former didn't, but the latter did. Drilled him twice in the gluteus maximus. He was carted off, squealing like a little girl.

The hooligan, nabbed and subsequently convicted with our testimony, served five years for armed robbery. In retrospect, I will always be thankful my father had slipped away earlier, after supervising the dinner rush. He would have pummeled the perp to a pulp, possibly placing his own life in jeopardy.

Pops looms from a clan of bold, honorable men: guys who are not only physically strong, but brave and wise as well. Fellas who routinely sacrifice to do the right thing. They know their good example as fathers, sons, and husbands, is crucial. They adhere to a code of principles notably visible with war veterans -- as is he.

Mother insisted I sleep with her that night, grateful I survived my brush with death. Alas, I was clueless, so her gesture evoked no significance at all until years later when *I* became a mother.

CHAPTER 17

I stand, amble over to a country French china cabinet displaying a 5" x 7" picture of my parents' wedding anniversary. Lifting the gold-leafed wood frame, I touch my forefinger to my lips and then convey the peck to the pic.

The oven's *ding-ding-ding* snaps me back to the puffy, soft round bread ball expanding in the oven. After kneading the dough about three minutes, I form it into a loaf, transfer it to a greased pan and let it rise until doubled in bulk -- another hour.

I traipse to the mailbox to retrieve *The Des Moines Dispatch*, sprinting back inside to avoid the first drops from a morning rain shower. I drop down onto a kitchen stool and peruse the front page. I'm astonished to read an "AMBER Alert" -- suspected child abduction bulletin -- was issued last night regarding Lily's disappearance. She is seventeen years old, legitimately qualifying for the activation, but the announcement catches me by surprise. The headline makes it all the more real. province

I extend a hand into my purse, the straps suspended from an iron chair-back spindle, and withdraw olive wood rosary beads from Medjugorje, a province located in the southwestern region of Bosnia-Herzegovina. To date, six young visionaries claim the Blessed Virgin Mary has appeared almost daily for thirty years, entrusting them with ten secrets relating to future events. When all ten secrets are revealed to all six peasants, chastisements will begin, affecting the Catholic Church and the world. These acts are slated to originate during the lifetimes of the oracles.

Apparently Our Lady of Peace requests we pray the rosary, convert others to The Lord, and fast, which could diminish the punishment for humanity. Fasting -- a spiritual discipline -- is defined as abstinence from food and drink for a period of time.

When combined with prayer, allegedly the Holy Spirit can transform your life.

I no sooner make the sign of the cross, when Rocco rings in.

"Maria, too early?"

"No way, I'm a vampire. I don't need much sleep. Wassup?"

"Hey, sista. Good news..."

CHAPTER 18

"*What* good news, Rocco?" I plead.

"Lily is home, safe and sound." He relays the update with certainty and energy in his voice.

I bow my head, then continue. "Will she be ok? Was she assaulted? Did you make any arrests?" I bombard him, contemplating and fearing the lifelong trauma she may suffer from her experience.

"You ask a lot of questions, Maria. Now, to answer them: yes, yes, and yes. We scored a tip from a reliable source and wasted no time issuing an arrest warrant. Think we'll be taking this brute to the big house down town."

"You rock, Rocco."

"Whatever. Hey, how'd your date go last night? Did you start any fires your man couldn't put out?"

"You know boss, let's just say *I* put out, and leave it at that." There was a pregnant pause.

"Dirty girl! Wish I could talk longer, but got to fly, Maria. I'm already late for roll call. Buzz you in a bit."

I know roll call will be followed by a briefing: daily assignments, info on recent crimes, descriptions of missing or wanted persons, and notifications from previous shifts. I figure I have some time to kill.

My gaze deviates toward the oven, seconds before it is set to *ding*. I don't want to disturb the raised dough, so I program the temperature to 350 degrees for 30 minutes. The bread should be done baking about the time Chip gets up for school.

No sooner have I hung up from Rocco, the phone again.

"Sweetie, how are you?" Good friend Emma is checking in from Chicago. Recently her husband was transferred with Brunswick Bowling, so she and the fam tore off for a new destiny and new digs.

"I miss you, Maria. Girls here are *soooo* conservative. Hell, I can't even sneak a drag from someone's smokes, cuz no one smokes. Sometimes you need to live a little on the edge. We certainly do."

"I hear that." We chat a few more minutes before her cell starts blowing up with calls, texts and emails.

"Emma, mark your calendar. Let's schedule a weekend at a B & B in Dubuque, that's about the half-way point between Des Moines and Chicago. What do ya say?"

"Book it, Dano!" she clamors. We cut off.

CHAPTER 19

Enthusiastic to share the bulletin about Lily, I scale the stairs two at a time, marching to Chip's bedroom. As soon as I secure the bow on my belted wrap-a-round white terrycloth robe, I breeze through his door -- despite the "Do Not Disturb" sign suspended from the doorknob -- then dally at the threshold.

There lies my boy, linens lassoing his legs, athletic shoes and shorts shunned onto the carpet. Surrounding him are trophies, ribbons, and team photos.

"Rise and shine, Junior." He was baptized Michael J, Magliani, after his father, though we nicknamed him Chip. I edge across the floor to his bed. He awakens to a blitzkrieg of roaring thunder and pulsating lightening as sprinkles blotch the skylight.

"Morning, Mom." He rubs his face, tries to focus, then peeks at the clock on the sideboard. "Kinda early." He scans splatters on the windowpane. "What's the forecast, anyway? I've got a game at 4:00 p.m. today."

"Oh, it's time to get your fanny out of bed. As far as the weather, I think you're lookin' at it. Will you have soccer if it's raining?" I wonder aloud, while planting my bum down beside him.

"Most definitely. But, if the lightening continues -- game off."

"Good to know," I nod. "Talked to Rocco this morning and he divulged some news about Lily."

"Cool. Hope it's good."

Chip glances away, almost intentionally refusing to look me in the eye. Certainly he's concerned, though he appears disingenuous. He seems almost struck by an attack of conscience, like he's playing tug-of-war whether or not to confide in me.

My cell shrills. It's Rocco calling me back. I nudge Chip, raise a finger in the air to signal I will be a minute.

"Hey, Maria. Kickin' some ass now. Feels like we've been injected with a jolt of adrenaline."

"Attaboy, Rocco. By the way, just curious, *who* was your 'reliable source' in finding Lily and apprehending the kidnapper?"

Hopefully I have gained his trust and he will disclose info related to the case. After all, the department recruited me, not vice versa.

"Maria, thought you knew," exclaims Rocco.

"It was *Chip.*"

CHAPTER 20

"Chip tipped you off, Rocco? When? What did *he* know that no one else did?" My eyes fixate on my son, lying in his bed, facing forward with a shitty grin.

"Maria, it went down like this:

"Lily had been kidnapped and was constrained by her attacker in a van in a rectory in Ames. After molesting her several times and assuming the dope was wearing off, her captor twisted toward an interior side pocket of the vehicle, clutching to dispense another vial of GHB.

With presence of mind, Lily channeled her mystic might and slammed a martial arts side-kick full into his face. Blood and bones. The unsuspecting assailant blasted through the van's side door, left unlatched, crumpling to the pavement.

Lily scrambled to the driver's seat, started the motor, rammed it into reverse and plowed through the closed garage door. She yanked her cell from the center console, switched it on and pressed speed-dial #9, connecting instantly to best friend Nataliya Chenko -- Chip's girlfriend and Lily's Crossfit partner. Needless to say, Nataliya buzzed Chip, who in turn, called us at about 2:00 a.m."

Rocco recounts the skirmish well, though my jaw hangs agape from the terrifying experience.

"But Rocco, if Lily was in possession of her cell the entire time, why couldn't you hone in on her earlier?" It's a given that I'm no electronics geek, but, seriously, what the hell's the purpose of GPS?

"Stay with me, Maria, I'll explain. Lily's mobile was in the van, but her abuser had clicked it *OFF*. You can't track a cell that is shut down or has a dead battery. Fortunately the phone was still charged, so when Lily flipped it *ON*, immediately we were able to trace the signal."

"By the way, Rocco, how big is this guy? The assaulter? I mean, what supernatural powers did

Lily rely on?" Arguably, she has strong, muscular legs from her body-shaping program and drill team, but, really? I bite my lip, though maybe I should bite my tongue.

"Damn girl, do we have a 'doubting Thomas' in our midst? Don't you ever watch the Discovery Channel? A little guy or a petite lady single-handedly lifting a car in an emergency? Maria, with the right mind set and a life-threatening situation, a person can lift 3000 pounds or more."

"I'll give you that, Rocco. By the way, where did you finally meet up with Lily? At the fraternity? Was she hurt? Did she drive back to the parking lot?" I drill my cousin.

"And lastly, *who* the fuck did you arrest?"

CHAPTER 21

Chip springs up to dress for school. I motion to him that I'm en route downstairs, in response to the *ding-ding-ding* emitting from the kitchen. I cancel the timer, transfer the steamy loaf from oven-to-rack to cool, before positioning Pecan Pumpkin Butter from Williams-Sonoma, next to the cutting board.

"First things first." Rocco continues, "Lily will live. She's got a lot of guts. We did apprehend a suspect in her disappearance, or *alleged* kidnapping, but we need to play by-the-book to land this sicko behind bars for a long, long time."

"Bro, throw me a bone!" I beg. I know my cousin. He's a first-rate detective and he would have taken all necessary precautions in recovering: prints, hair, blood, clothing, paint chips, tire tracks -- evidence to eventually convict. Right now I just hanker for a name.

"Actually, Maria, we intercepted Lily after her escape, and directed her back to the original crime scene -- the fraternity parking lot. We needed her statement and any insights she had to aid our investigation. We are also interested if this is an isolated incident. In addition, we transported her to Assumption Hospital to administer a rape kit."

My heart leaps to my throat. I swallow hard. My, how life can change in the course of one night.

"Rocco, will Lily undergo therapy?" I'm well aware that rape victims are likely candidates for depression, PTSD, drug abuse, and suicide.

"I would expect a tough road ahead. Being surrounded by a loving, supportive family and friends are key in her recovery."

"Jesus, boss, so who's in custody? A frat brother? A maintenance man? A random stalker or just some scum-sucking pig?" I respect Rocco's position, but I want clued in.

"Ok, I know what you're after, Maria," Rocco remarks, attempting to calm my increasing frustration. "Our suspect, sitting in jail as we speak,

is a thirty-five-year-old, uh, hmm, Catholic priest --
Father Paul Fulitano."

Once he starts stammering, I pick up on the
hesitation in his voice. "Come on, cuz, what's the
dealio?" I demand.

Rocco continues, "I stand corrected...Father Paul
impersonated a priest."

CHAPTER 22

"What the fuck! Are you saying some punk-bitch pedophile, *impersonating* a priest, kidnapped and molested Lily?"

"Dial it down, Maria, we're just now figuring it all out. Matter of fact we need to get together. You available tomorrow afternoon?"

"Damn straight. Is this part of our covert affairs?"

"Bingo. How about we meet at the Coffee Clutch around the corner from Immaculate Mary, say, about 2:30?"

"Roger that."

* * *

Luckily my business is concluded for the day. I met earlier with Jason, my contractor and ceramics guy, the plumber, and Craig, an awesome Aussie painter, the newest addition to our expanding team. We discussed progress to date, then assigned responsibilities and listing expectations. The quaint cottage was in store for a ritzy reno.

While the wide hickory planks pegged for the living space are back-ordered, the twelve-inch glazed burnished tiles for the bathroom and kitchen floors are ready for installation. The ceiling and the walls can then be prepared for paint. The plumber can now connect the water lines. A successful morning.

* * *

Clancy and I agreed to rally uptown for lunch at Mannella's for pizza by the slice. It's a strip-mall eatery, tricked out in Tuscan décor -- a back-drop of wrought-iron shelves displaying earth-tone jars, urns, bowls, framed-art, floral and fruit greenery. Little Italy from Armani to Prada -- head to toe. I arrive first and ask for outdoor seating.

When Clancy finally shows, he leans over the round café parlor table and plants a deep, hot smooch on my lips with his tongue swirling -- which I think makes the kiss French, not Italian. No doubt my rosy-stained cheeks mirror my embarrassment.

"Hello to you too," I pant. "So, that's how it's gonna go, huh?"

"Maria, I'm revved from last night. Girl, you always gotta finish what you start."

He plunks down. Immediately his right hand goes fishing. It skims up my pink flirty gossamer skirt, resting on my knee. The man has the attention span of a gnat.

Our white apron-clad waiter serves a bottle of San Pellegrino, a mineral water with natural carbonation, along with a "Bouquetiere Pizza" -- a fusion of fresh seasonal veggies atop a thin square-cut whole wheat crust. The "fare of the day" includes tomatoes, carrots, zucchini, yellow squash, pearl onions and peas sautéed in butter and sugar, speckled with lemon pepper and sweet basil. Okay, I admit to my nickname -- *menu mouth*.

Following the feast, Clancy and I nip cups of espresso spiked with shots of Grappa, an Italian brandy consisting of distilled pressed grape skins, stems, seeds and pulp, leftover from winemaking. The brew might be more intoxicating than I realized, because in my frisky state, I flip off one sandal and rub my bare foot up Clancy's leg, scraping toes against skin. His wiry curly hair piques certain points in me.

He squeezes my hand. "Maria, you sexy babe, we got to bounce."

I sense sexual energy coursing through his veins too.

Clancy pays the bill while I journey toward the Ladies Room to re-apply shimmer to my lips and spritz Coach Poppy Perfume round my neck and beneath my skirt -- recalling the Girl Scouts Motto: "Be Prepared."

My man may have similar notions when he texts: *"Meet me at my car. We can ride together to my place for indoor games."*

That's what I'm talkin' about.

CHAPTER 23

I exit the cafe and scope the parking lot for the blue XKE. Aware of a high-pitched whistle, I crane my neck toward an alley adjacent to Mannella's, where deliveries are made. There stands Clancy, luring me with a *come hither* gesture. After hiking over to him, he links my arm and steers me further behind the building.

He braces me up against a brick-façade wall, stretches my tank top down, and with his wet supple lips, starts sucking my breasts. At the same time, he spreads my legs with his knee, then slides aside my low-rise lavender thong to accommodate the "Boy Scout's Sign" -- the two finger salute. Joe Mama! Note to self: *Little boys get impatient; big boys wait for nothing!*

"Maria, please come home with me, now."

Clancy picks up my hand and coaxes me toward his car. Indeed it is time to go. I appreciate that we possibly escaped a citation for: *Inappropriate display of affection.*

We tool to his abode -- the fourth-story of an historic eighty-year-old warehouse loft located on the greenbelt, flanking the Des Moines River. The proximity is awesome for Saturday Farmers' Market, restaurants, bars and the Cathedral only a few blocks away -- for confessing misdeeds.

Clancy has customized the space with cherry cabinets and hardwood floors, stainless steel appliances, and black granite counters. Industrial describes the character of his digs with high ceilings, exposed ductwork, encased over-sized windows, all in a minimalistic style. Tough, I think, snuggling up to steel and glass.

However, he has softened the tone with colorful plump pillows, a brown and ivory Safari runner and a stunning vertical fusion-glass tile backsplash below the kitchen cabinets.

"Welcome, Maria," he closes the front door, crosses the room, and opens the entry to the master bedroom suite. A vintage king-size four-poster, situated atop a plush white sheepskin rug, anchors the room. Black-lacquered nightstands and a high-boy contrast well with the surroundings. What appears to be a swanky spa-bathroom connects off the closet.

Clancy sweeps me up, breathless with anticipation, and plucks me down on the bed. He peels off my clothes while stripping himself nude. The man is well-endowed and hard to look away from.

"I've been thinking about this for a long while, Maria. Please don't make me wait any longer."

I honestly think he would cry if I deny him now.

"Clancy, have at it."

* * *

...Bless me Father, for I have sinned.

CHAPTER 24

Following "Afternoon Delight" with Clancy, we hop into his car, rolling back to Mannella's. I bid adieu and set off to attend Chip's soccer game. Unexpectedly the rain subsides and blue swells the skies, so I drop the top on my late model British Racing Green BMW. I punch in the Michael Jackson "Thriller" CD and crank up the volume.

My sister Jenny phoned earlier and we agreed to meet up at the stadium for the semi-final match with the Valley Juncture Warriors. I lug two red-and-white padded seat cushions inscribed with *Saints*.

"Hey, sweetie, that's the spirit!" mouths Jenny as she hugs me, before settling in for the game. "You look...a little disheveled. What have you been up to, Maria?"

I swear nothing gets by her. And considering she also inherited the same crappy eye disease as 88 other family members, that's some sight, sista.

"Actually, it's been a very productive day. Epic, in fact. Let's see: baked bread, jogged twenty minutes on the treadmill, conferred with my contractor on the renovation, did lunch, and, oh yeah, *did* Clancy."

"Whoa, back-up. That last part, did *what*? You know I need the deets."

Jenny has been married forever to high-school sweetheart, Pierce (definitely a money-name) so a little thrill now and again, vicariously through me, seems harmless.

"Munched lunch at Mannella's, then sprinted to Clancy's for coffee and conversation."

"R-i-g-h-t. Coffee?" She contests, "Come on Maria, let's be candid. Remember, I've seen the guy in the flesh. At the pool, anyway. As I recall he's hung... like a moose."

My sis easily conquers grit and guts. Above all else, she triumphs with the truth.

"You know, I'm good with that visual," endorsing her assessment.

We jump up, slaughter the "Star Spangled Banner," then encourage Chip by hollering when he runs the full length of the field in jersey #16, only to miss his kick on goal.

Jenny and I continue chatting throughout the game, while scarfing down a bucket of popcorn and chugging lemonade. We cackle, dish the dirt, and share opinions on politics and religion -- we'd already covered sex.

My cell trills.

"Hey Maria, wondered if you'd do me a favor."

CHAPTER 25

He seems upset; his voice is cracking. "Of course, Rocco. If I can."

"Lily's parents are refusing for her to fill a script for 'Plan B One-Step' – the emergency contraceptive. She has seventy-two hours after unprotected sex to take the one-pill medication. Because of her devout background, and according to her mom, the morning-after tablets are deemed sinful. Do you believe that crap? Can you intervene, Maria?"

I tap Jenny on the shoulder, point to the phone, then clatter down the stadium stairs for privacy.

"Christ, Rocco, you're pretty much crossing the line here, aren't you? I mean, with confidentiality issues and the family's religious stance?" He's generally in control at all times. This is so uncharacteristic.

"Maria, I've had it with her folks. Especially her mother. I swear she's batshit crazy. Lily doesn't deserve to suffer any more, primarily with a pregnancy-by-rape. Her parents are out of touch and this simple course of action could relieve anxiety and halt the risk of a life-long stigma."

"Cuz, I heartily agree with you. But, you need to zip it up and play nice. The decision is not yours. I'll discuss things with Lily and her mom and dad, but only if the Police Chief approves it first."

Granted, Rocco and I are both practicing Catholics, though with our faith, practice doesn't necessarily make perfect. I've been accused of approaching Catholicism with a *smorgasbord attitude* -- picking doctrines I like and passing over those I don't. Case in point: I oppose abortion, though I condone birth control and emergency contraception -- preventing ovulation, fertilization, and inhibiting implantation.

"Gotcha," Rocco bellows. "Check with you later, Maria. Thanks."

I disconnect and dash back to the game. Apparently our *Saints,* with Chip at the helm, have taken a 1-0 lead in the second half with a corner kick. Only five minutes remain, so Jennie shoves off.

I hang around long enough to congratulate Chip and the team for the win, then decide to leave also, eager to blast home and research the subject. I rewind mental tapes concerning "Plan B" and the possibility of its use with Lily. Before leaving the parking lot however, I scour my cell's contact list, scroll down, and call a friend of a friend, for Father's number at Holy Mother of Gd Church office.

"Father, this is Maria Magliani, over at St. Monica's parish. We were introduced about a month ago at an MS fundraiser at Veterans Auditorium." I hope he remembers me otherwise I will have to start from scratch with the research.

"Of course, Maria. Your son attends Immaculate Mary. You're the Sherlock Holmes aficionado."

"Close enough. Cousin Rocco is the Holmes buff and my partner-in-crime. He's a detective with the Des Moines Police Department, but, you're on the right track. Father, I'm in desperate need of the most up-to-date verdict on the morning-after pill and the Catholic Church. I know you've recently been ordained and you have your ear to the ground on policy."

I've heard that today's young novitiates are quite the opposite of liberal. I hold my breath and cross my fingers awaiting his reply.

"Well, Maria, we've never fluctuated in our opposition to 'Plan B' and its' generic, 'Next Choice'."

Oh, dear, I think we're screwed. I start my engine and steer into the slow traffic lane.

"But, Father, what is the Church's stand in the case of *rape?*"

CHAPTER 26

"In the case of rape," Father Kermit begins, "there remains a moral dilemma dispensing 'Plan B' in U.S. Catholic hospitals. Yet, the federal government has mandated that option must be available to these victims."

I screech to a halt and pull the Beamer over.

"I'm sorry, Father, I'm confused. So, the morning after pills *are* allowed -- for rape only?" I want the definitive answer on this matter. My word, my reputation rests on it.

Fr. Kermit corrects me with an emphatic, "No! These pills may disturb a fertilized egg by releasing a steroid ingredient which impedes implantation. An attack on the environment or womb could prevent survival. We believe an ovum is already a child of God. No matter *how* it was impregnated, it's a tiny human being. Therefore, aborting it would be murderous. Nonetheless, we are obligated to offer 'Plan B'."

"Really, Father? Murder?" Pressure peaks. As far as Rocco -- Officer Bad Ass -- fitful with frustration, well, he will positively come unglued with this update.

"Maria, life begins at conception. Interfering with that event violates the Fifth Commandment: 'Thou shalt not kill.' If it's any comfort, the probability of a pregnancy resulting from rape is extremely rare. The physical trauma itself reduces its incidence, along with the age of the woman, the time of the month, sterile women, sterile men, the percentage of women taking birth control, and the percentage who will miscarry. And finally, those who do become pregnant can elect adoption. These are the facts; this is our faith."

"Thank you. I appreciate your clarification, Father."

I waste no time dialing my own parish priest, the Catholic Council, and Assumption Hospital for further enlightenment. No cigar.

Chip texts me that he will head home after a shower at school, so I roar toward Gray's Lake for a twenty-minute run on the circle trail. That should allow me enough time to air out the cobwebs in my noggin and develop a dinner design -- unless of course, I decide to skinny dip and play hooky instead.

CHAPTER 27

After sautéing chopped onions, garlic, bacon bits, and hamburger, I drain the grease, then combine Italian spices, a smidgen of sugar, and canned crushed plum tomatoes. My prepared quick-sauce will be ready to ladle over buttered bow-tie pasta in about a half-hour. Sliced whole-wheat bread will accompany an iceberg-lettuce salad, dolloped with feta cheese and Mom's homemade vinaigrette dressing. My moniker: Make it fast; eat it faster.

* * *

"So, honey, how was school?"

Chip clears his plate and thrusts it in the dishwasher.

"Pretty good, Mom. Thanks for showing up at the game. That was a big deal -- winning the semis."

He wipes the counters before sprawling on the kitchen bench.

"You look a little bummed. Something wrong?" I probe.

He shrugs. "Matter of fact, I'm waiting for a callback from Rocco."

Instantly anticipation hangs in the air.

"Can you talk about it?" I don't want to invade my son's liaison relationship with Rocco and the police, though Chip concerns me with his glazed stare. He stands, shuffles over to his gym bag and digs out a legal-size white sealed envelope marked: *WATCH OUT!* in thick black caps.

"What's this? And where did it come from?"

He crinkles his nose, just like his dad used to do.

At first, I strive to stall my composure. Once my knees begin buckling however, I commence shaking with a rush of worry. Next, I become intrigued.

"It's cool, Mom. I found it crammed in a side compartment of my bag with my water bottle. I haven't opened it because it's not addressed to me. Thought I might run it by Rocco first."

Smart kid, my son. I hunger to examine the letter and its contents. Considering I'm a Certified Graphoanalyst -- one who scientifically identifies the character and personality of a writer through handwriting -- I yearn to scrutinize the slant, size and spacing of strokes. In addition, I would pay particular attention to the pressure used and other details which would readily reveal countless traits of the author.

I remember that I will be meeting Rocco at 2:30 p.m. tomorrow, so I toddle off to my room, and flop on the bed to await evening developments.

The phone.

"Hey Clancy, what's up?" Damn, I truly hope he's calling about getting together later.

"Maria, I'm hankering for a Cold Stone creation. A cone or a custom sundae with sprinkles, candy shavings, whipped crème and nuts, drizzled with syrup. You game?"

Oh, boy, the heat we create together would most definitely melt any ice cream concoction.

"Yummy. I'd love to. Pick me up?"

"Sure, babe, leaving now. See you in fifteen."

CHAPTER 28

I dart to the bathroom for a speed-shower -- certain
to purify all pulse points -- then spritz Coach Poppy
cologne around my head, wrists, and *wherever.* Might
as well stink good. With the weather uncommonly
warm in Des Moines, I wriggle into a sleeveless
leopard-print ruched dress, constructed with a
gathering technique to highlight feminine curves
and swerves. The cowl neckline with its loose-fitting
fold-over fabric, flatters every cup size. Black ballet
flats, mascara, ruby lips, and I'm good to go.

Chip calls out that he will be in his room studying, so I breeze over and say goodnight. He promises to inform me when he hears back from Rocco regarding the suspicious envelope discovered his gym bag.

Just as I peek out the dining room bay window and spot Clancy pulling up the drive, my cell *beeps* with a new voicemail: *"Hey, Maria, thinking about you lately. Gimme a call."*

I recognize the digits. The message is from Frankie. Oh dear, trouble city. Returning *that* call would be a big mistake -- huge mistake. At the same time, I'm curious what he might have on his mind. Ok, I know what's always on his mind.

I sprint out to Clancy, duck down and crumple into the XKE seat.

"Nice dress," he remarks. "Easy to get on and off."

"T-h-a-n-k-s. I was under the impression we were zipping out for ice cream treats." Admittedly, my provocative outfit may have side-lined Clancy's good intentions.

"Maria, let me explain something," he elaborates. "Cheetah, tiger, fox, any animal skin -- faux or otherwise -- is a turn-on for guys. You must know we think we're the king of the jungle. Well, babe, you're the jungle. Especially rockin' that garb."

"Good to know, Professor Higgins."

We cruise for a few blocks before hauling into a neighborhood park. After scouting out a secluded site, he positions the vehicle so he can observe everything nearby. Clancy bends in. Curling his fingers from both hands around my collar, he tugs me in. At once his left hand slithers up my skirt, delving deeper. His right hand draws down the cowl neck, exposing braless breasts. His lips follow.

His phone rings.

"Fire Marshall McClavey," transmits a voice over the Bluetooth stereo speakers, "we have a two-alarm fire in the burbs in Clive. Flames appear to be radiating from the epicenter of a twenty-bay strip-mall at 6915 Francis Avenue. You're needed on-site ASAP. Are you available? If so, what's your ETA?"

"Affirmative. Eight minutes," Clancy calls out. Immediately he presses the pedal to the metal, pulls a uie and speeds me home. "Sorry, babe," he mouths and at the same time he motions for me to vacate the car. No ice cream, but at least my virginity remains intact.

He extends his arm into the back bucket and accesses a portable Kojak -- a red rotating flashing light, which he affixes to his roof top before rolling away.

I sashay inside and contemplate listening to a Kindle download, *The House of Silk: A Sherlock Holmes Novel*, by Anthony Horowitz, written in the style of Arthur Conan Doyle. This is the first and only new tale authorized by the Conan Doyle Estate.

I notify Chip that I'm back. Faint conversation ripples in the background -- presumably he and girlfriend Nataliya are sharing sweet exchanges.

The doorbell chimes.

CHAPTER 29

"Hey, Maria." Rocco steps in and without hesitation wraps his arms around me.

"Nice surprise. I know we're meeting up tomorrow," I signal by pointing from Rocco to me, "so are you here for Chip?"

"Yeah, wanted to confiscate the evidence he found at school, concealed in his bag." He tosses his head, and lifts his shoulder -- conceivably downplaying the importance of the find.

"Ok, what's your take on the note?"

"You know, Maria, without checking it out first, I don't want to comment."

"Of course, I know. I'm worried about Chip." Choking back tears I wonder, have I placed him in harm's way?

Rocco squeezes my hand, and then tucks my chin to his chest.

"Come on cuz, you think I'd let anything happen to my godson? Chip's safety my prime concern."

"You're a good man, Rocco. Does Eden know how lucky she is?" I refer to his wife of eight years. The guy has boogied the bridal boardwalk a few times previous, but, we all knew Eden was *the one*. Immediately my thoughts fly to Sherlock Holmes and his romantic interest in Irene Adler -- *the woman*.

"Smooth, Maria. Hey, did you find out any new altering-info after talking with your clergy know-it-all about 'Plan B'?" He raises his hand up flat in front of my face, in a surrender gesture. "Don't worry, I've calmed down considerably," he promises, obviously softening his attack on Lily's Mom and Pop.

"Sorry, dude, the word is no-go. No emergency contraception pill for Lily. Not according to the Catholic Church, anyway. I did visit with her parents, after clearing it with your Police Chief. Lily's risk of pregnancy-by-rape is small, so let's wish her well and hope for the best."

Right. I recollect Rocco is never good at wishin' and hopin'. For Christ's sake, how many cops are?

He bites his lip and clenches his jaw.

"Appreciate your assistance, Maria. Think I'll go scout out Chip. Is he upstairs?" He lifts his head and raises his eyebrows.

"Yep, should be in his room."

* * *

From the top of the staircase I hear, "Maria, would you come here?"

I know the voice is Rocco's; his *tone,* however, scares the shit out of me!

CHAPTER 30

I mount the stairs, two at a time to Chip's room, while my heart thumps in my head, in my throat, in my chest. Rocco corners me at the bedroom door and grips my hand, directing me toward a desk chair.

"Maria, sit down. I'm sorry if I alarmed you." Rocco surely can see fear in my face. "Chip has just alerted me to inappropriate conduct by a coach in the boys' locker room at school." He glances at my son, whose eyes gloss over.

"You, Chip? You were victimized?" I query, as my gaze zips from Rocco to my son.

"No way, Mom, I swear!" he snaps emphatically. "But a few of my soccer teammates admitted they were, and I feel terrible for them." Chip eases up from the edge of his bed, and begins pacing. "I feel guilty because I wasn't singled out. Does that make sense?"

I drift over to Chip to hold his hand, while rubbing his back. Honestly, I'm speechless.

"Sport," Rocco confides, "this is a predictable reaction. You wonder why you were spared and your friends suffered. Sorry pal, sex offenders seek out specific targets for a variety of reasons."

"What do ya mean, Rocco?" Chip asks, biting his fingernail.

"Well, often times predators tend to select youngsters who are lonely and quiet, passive -- some, even starved for attention. The victims usually exhibit low self-esteem and low self-confidence. They may choose a mark with few friends or siblings, or one who hails from a dysfunctional family. That's not you, man. You don't fit the mold." Rocco engulfs my son with a two-arm bear hug.

"Also," I add, "abusers are masters of façade. They start off enticing their prey with extreme kindness, showering gifts on them – electronics, clothes, pumped up kicks -- presents to help gain compliance and build trust. Nonetheless, eventually they want *one* thing, and will do anything to lead the lamb to slaughter."

"Your mom's right. I've heard about handouts of cash to facilitate drug purchases. It's easy to get sucked into their lair; it's hard to get out. Eighty percent of perpetrators are people we already know and believe in -- a neighbor, a teacher, a minister, or a coach. Anyone with exposure to young people must be suspect," Rocco warns.

"Did the other players confide in you, Chip? What did they say? How many are involved?"

"Maria," Rocco announces, "I need to scoot back to headquarters with this new evidence." He holds the inscribed envelope in the air and waves goodbye. "I'll let myself out, guys. See you tomorrow Maria, at 2:00 p.m. for coffee."

Rocco bolts, leaving Chip and me to resume our heart-to-heart.

"Mom, my friend Jeremiah is one of the casualties. So's Travis. Why would they consent…to being exploited?" Chip drags his forearm across his eyes, wiping away tears, but leaving behind the stain of life's experience.

"Sweetie, we're out of my expertise range, though I would guess the predator's hook is more about manipulation, power and control, than consensus. The victims are often left tormented by shame and guilt. Many times they resort to self-loathing, and sad to say, even suicide. It's a vicious cycle. I'm optimistic that counseling will help repair the emotional damage ingrained by your coach."

"Come here, Mom." Chip motions me over to sit on the bed. I sidle next to him. "I need you to know that I'm thankful I wasn't molested. And, I'm grateful you are always here for me -- I can count on you. Sometimes, though, like now, I really miss Dad."

He didn't need to say more. "I know honey. Me too."

Instantly the ceiling fan above us begins whirling around without assistance from the wall switch.

"Yet, Chip, in some ways I feel Dad is always with us."

CHAPTER 31

Wow, kids grow up fast these days. I don't remember knowing about or ever discussing sexual abuse in my childhood -- let alone luring young boys with sports equipment, lottery tickets and trips to paradise. Sometimes I want to return to the good ole days where ignorance *was* bliss.

* * *

I slip into a pink-and-white polka dot nightie with a flared ruffled hem, cognizant Clancy might not call, following his firefighter caper. Unfamiliar with inferno protocol, it seemed odd when the dispatcher contacted him, knowing it was his day off. Apparently Fire Marshalls are most definitely in demand -- or at least *my* Fire Marshall.

I settle in with Kindle and Sherlock Holmes, *The House of Silk*. The story begins with a visit from a prominent art dealer imploring Holmes' and Watson's assistance in curbing an international conspiracy, threatening the sheer fabric of society.

I slide *ON* to initiate the eBook just as my cell rings.

"Hey, Jason," I perk up, eager to resolve any renovation issues concerning the Cedar Ridge project.

"Maria, wanted to touch base with you on our progress at the condo."

Jason, a friendly easygoing guy with a sense of humor, is flirty and sexy too. I enjoy when he relays his misadventures from the singles' scene. He's around my age, early forties, but a confirmed bachelor with one thing on his mind, (well, maybe two) -- flying solo. At present, he's batting 1000 by sidestepping commitment and the wedding waltz.

"Of course, how we lookin'?"

"Well, I hope we might meet and settle up with expenses; I have receipts totaling around $11,000. I've paid the subs out-of-pocket, so I need to...um, git r done," he stammers.

"Absolutely." Damn, we are breezing right through the makeover money. However, I reason, the faster I complete the project, the sooner I can collect rental fees. "I have a conflict tomorrow. What about Friday?"

"Cool, Maria. Sorry to press you, but the recession has drained all my resources. These crews insist on being paid daily -- or at least by the job."

"No worries," I reassure him. "I appreciate you running interference. I'll buzz you after checking my calendar."

I disconnect, then lob the cell across the bed. I feel toasted -- had a full day, craving a quiet night. No such luck. My phone beeps with a text: *"Sis, Gina and I want you and Chip to come for dinner soon. What day works?"*

The memo arrives from brother Nick and his wife. My siblings have showered us with love and support since Michael's death. The police report listed: "Suicide by Firearm; due to gun wound to head with .38 caliber handgun" as the immediate cause of death. But to this day the verdict is still out, at least in my mind. Not to the method used, but to the malefactor. Fortunately my family converged on us with encouragement and particularly as role models for my impressionable son.

I commence texting a response to Nick about a future date, when I'm interrupted with another call. Glimpsing down, I groan.

Shit! It's Frankie again.

CHAPTER 32

"Maria, what's up, girl?"

Admittedly, Frankie has crossed my mind a time or two, primarily in a scandalous apparition. I recall the impression left on my neck by his hot breath, when I reminisce about his voracious love-making. Never could get his fill. His handwriting reveals indulgence in sensual pleasures -- that which appeals to the eyes, ears, nose, and sense of touch -- as suggested by heavy, muddy writing with corrugated strokes.

Similarly, studies have shown that other powerful successful men also tend to share these same traits:

ambition, persistence, self-reliance, and an enduring positive attitude. Yep, that'd be Frankie. And Clancy. And my late husband, Michael. Right; now, what does that say about me?

"Frankie, it's all good." He'd be the last person I'd confide in. "How's it hangin'?" Crap, poor choice of words. I resume again. "How's life at the Pirelli compound?"

His family manages a trash and waste removal company in Des Moines. He's the youngest son in a menagerie with six brothers and sisters, undeniably plagued by hormone and testosterone levels off the chart.

I met Frankie, the make-out king, in high school where he became my first serious boyfriend -- the love of my life, albeit to that point in time. We were inseparable. Spent hours French-kissing, wet and wicked, in his International Scout, parked a few blocks from my home. I remember exchanging Christmas gifts senior year. I bought him a red cable-knit sweater; he bought me a gold chain with a suspended locket, that when opened, revealed a timepiece. I have it buried in a box beneath love letters and snapshots in a trunk in the attic. Eventually he played me like a piano when I left for college and he dumped me for a girl who would go all the way.

Frankie admits to sleeping with her forty-six times before she got knocked up and they *had* to get married. Yeah, that doesn't happen anymore. Now if you do conceive, a tiny yellow tablet makes it all go bye-bye -- along with, as the saying goes: *the consequences of your actions.*

"Maria, kinda thinkin' we might wine and dine together sometime soon. You game? Oh, hold up. You joined at the hip with fire boy?"

"Let's say we're in the discovery phase."

"Yeah, I remember. That was my favorite," he genuinely moans.

Hmmm, instantly I remember too. Frankie had been an awesome kisser -- I twinge as I imagine the rush I got from his soft kisses.

"Ok, Frankie, let me figure out my calendar and get back to you."

Have mercy, Lord, for I am weak.

CHAPTER 33

After texting brother Nick and contractor Jason about agendas, I sift through real estate bookwork and bills. Apparently losing interest quickly, my attention dissolves into daydreaming about the men in my life.

First, but not foremost, frisky Frankie looms. At seventeen he was my first sweetheart. He demonstrated affection and intimacy, for which I will forever be grateful. I achieved sensitivity and sensory expression with him -- holding hands, hugging, tickling, and sharing feelings.

I didn't love high school, though the memories are mostly good. Managing classes and homework daily, posed diligent days. Hosting and coat-checking at my father's steak house in the evenings, assured nonstop nights. Little time to stray into much mischief. "An idle mind is the devil's workshop." I guess I was too harried frolicking in my garden of make-believe, thereby keeping the reality devil at bay.

Lest we forget the Catholic Church's edict: perpetual potential to commit sin, without benefit of doing the deed. The mere fantasizing of sexual contact tallies as a strike in the *not gravely immoral* camp. Example: if a guy even checks out a hot chick and contemplates -- I wanna tap that -- he will be schlepping the confessional column come Saturday morn for his transgression. Next, the enduring guilt. I've gone on record theorizing that's why women can't enjoy sex -- the guilt. From day one. Unless we're procreating, *the deed* does us dirty. Damn that apple and Eve. She never had a chance to delight in the playground of carnal knowledge. Neither do we. About the time women begin to encounter good regular sex, we wind up -- pregnant, with a reputation as a slut, or forever branded with gonorrhea or syphilis, a modern day Scarlet Letter with a badge of blame to boot.

Freshman year in college I composed my first English class essay: "Is it better to have loved and lost, or never to have loved at all?" I defended the latter. If you had never loved, then you would never know what you had missed. Pencil in an idiot point. In hindsight, I would have opted for the experience. The value of a sizzling, torrid love affair: *Priceless*.

So, Frankie was my shining knight, until a more aggressive voluptuous maiden penetrated his armor by dribbling down her drawers. Shit happens. He and I have remained friends over the years, despite his three failed marriages. On occasion we have reconnected -- kindred spirits bumping in the night. Since life has rolled the dice, I (and Katy Perry) are often puzzled if he was "The One That Got Away."

Subsequently, Clancy makes the cut as a prominent beau on my list of suitors. Exciting, energetic, with a healthy sex drive, he has become an impressive diversion, a transitional partner since Michael. A classic black Magic 8-Ball may well reveal if our paths will simply cross, or cascade toward the future. In the meantime, I'll treasure the trip.

Be that as it may, my dearly-departed hubby trumps all contenders as *the* man in my life, though his absence has created a gaping hole. I jot down my thoughts:

I didn't miss you
when the sun banked
on the sand in Sarasota.
That happens every day.

I didn't miss your smile
on the slopes in Keystone
by myself
skiing on President's Day.

And Las Vegas cards
held no significance
for me
when I didn't see your face.

Apple-picking in Michigan
left no appeal
since I didn't miss your eyes –
however exceptional.

While biking the Bahamas, breathless
where we honeymooned
and you fulfilled me,
I failed to miss you.

But Spring in Chicago
with your family
reminded me of your gentle touch
and my heart ached.

And in Des Moines
home at last
where we won and lost it all –
I miss you.

CHAPTER 34

I awake to morning rays ascending mullioned panes of glass, causing my lids to flicker, squashing out day break. My attention draws toward a nearby drainpipe as goldfinch occupants sing in three-part harmony. With a furtive glance at the clock-radio on the sideboard, I exhale noisily, appreciating I'm bestowed a twenty-minute reprieve from tackling Thursday.

Suddenly I realize Clancy didn't phone nor come by after his fire fighter duties. Immediately I trace the Sign of the Cross on my head, chest and shoulders -- *In the name of the Father, and of the Son, and of the Holy Spirit, Amen* -- and recite the Holy Rosary, meditating on the Glorious Mysteries for those people possibly impacted by the blaze.

I wonder if *The Des Moines Dispatch* carries details regarding Clancy's inferno. I jog to the mailbox and withdraw the daily, but gasp when scanning the headlines: *"Where is Joey Gannon Today?"*

The front page displays a current digitally-generated-image of him and an update concerning the twelve-year-old boy's disappearance a year earlier, while delivering the Sunday edition of the newspaper.

Yikes! I remember the day Joey, a close cul-de-sac neighbor, vanished. I am stunned to acknowledge he remains missing. I had spotted him that morning at about 6:00 a.m. when he and his pooch Gertie cut a swath through my back yard, pulling a wagon, heading two blocks up the street to collect, roll, and distribute the weekend publication.

Since his disappearance, his parents, Judd and Nora, have painstakingly participated in incessant searches, frequent television interviews and appeals for their son's safe return. They printed and posted flyers, as well as consulting with various astrologers, mediums, and even several renowned psychics. In addition, Joey's mom succeeded in having his photo posted on milk cartons with other missing children.

To this day, the woman, plagued by sorrow and despair, has dedicated her complete existence toward her son's eventual homecoming. Godspeed.

The article surmises that Joey was seized and enslaved by a pedophile ring, possibly with Omaha connections. The story intimated that conceivably Nebraska law enforcement was associated with the abduction. To date, rumors have been scotched -- no Joey.

I smear away tears. Optimistically, Joey Gannon will be found soon, unharmed and delivered into the cradling arms of his family.

A Sherwood Forest horn Sound Font jolts me from the reverie, notifying me of a new text message: *"Hey, Maria, connect with you today at 2:30 at Coffee Clutch, around the corner from school. Accompanying me will be results from the note found in Chip's gym bag at school."*

"You're never gonna guess whose DNA we matched."

CHAPTER 35

"What the hell, Rocco? You're saying that fornicating porn-dog fake priest scribbled the threatening note to Chip? I prayed all night you had that prick locked up!"

"You know, Maria, this is a free country. Under current law, a defendant has an absolute right to bail -- the American justice system at its finest. Father Paul Vincensi, a.k.a. Spanky Collier, has a prior string of arrests for stalking and harassment, but he has never been formerly charged. At this juncture we booked him and then had to cut him lose. The mope wasted no time hightailing over to school to rendezvous with soccer coach, Jack Crew, before he was popped for molesting boys from his team."

"Perfect, I'm pretty pumped about our penal code. If we could just stay even with the bums. I swear Rocco, they're gainin' on us."

Arguably I know the USA has the best system going, but sometimes, even that falls short.

"Chill, girl, let's fixate on one issue at a time. For now it appears Chip was warned in the letter to stay out of the way of 'the powers that be' and their shenanigans."

An alarm signal sounds in my skull. I bite my lip and shoot Rocco a disapproving eye.

"What do you mean, *'warned'?*" Chip had not unsealed the envelope at our house, so I sit unaware of its contents.

"Don't worry, kiddo. We got it covered."

He fiddles with his cappuccino spoon, swirling whipped crème clouds in his coffee. Conceivably he is hopeful I will change the subject -- or he will.

"Get real, Rocco. You're out-ranked; I'm a mom. Telling me not to worry goes against my grain. Ain't gonna happen -- 'I Was Born This Way'." Damn, Rocco has no clue what I'm feeling. Even though he's married, he's not yet a father. For Christ's sake, I carried this kid in my belly for nine months before I ever met him. That's pretty fucking familiar. Unlikely I'll quit worrying about him on cue. What would his Dad say, with me putting Chip in harm's way?

* * *

Memories flood back, with father and son activities -- T-ball at Valerius Park, football in the backyard, tagging along to work with Michael to craft pizza faces and mini triple-decker deli sandwiches, tobogganing with the cousins, and trick-or-treating. A wedge of life...never again to be shared.

I recall one Lenten season when our parish priest urged school-aged tykes to assist others less fortunate by contributing change each week into a slotted cardboard carton to benefit missionaries. Michael was delighted to float the coinage to Chip after his completing his chores each Saturday, thereby teaching him charity. We didn't realize until Good Friday that Chip had borrowed from the mission money to buy me a birthday gift. Good call though, he left an IOU.

Along with meatless Fridays, another encouraged sacrificial Lenten act is to deny oneself a favorite food for the forty days and forty nights leading up to Easter. Chip's classmates proclaimed they would abstain from Skittles, M&M's, cookie-dough ice cream, and chocolate-covered marshmallow bunnies. Chip assured us he offered to forego *fruit*.

I fast-forward to our eight-year-old son, reporting to Michael, when he surprised the window washer hired from Craig's List. Apparently the handyman was seen sniffing my unmentionables from a highboy drawer in our bedroom. Ew! Really? God I hope they were *clean* undies.

* * *

"So Rocco, what else did you discern from the letter?"

"Nothing of any consequence, Maria. Idle threats mostly. We believe we've pretty much cleaned house -- what with the principal, soccer coach, and now the phony priest, ousted."

"All the same, since the faux father successfully finessed himself in and out of Chip's high school -- after first having been arrested and charged with rape -- well, the guy should at least be tailed." I shake my head, confused as to how Collier could ever have been approved by the diocese in the first place.

"You're quite opinionated, missy. Besides, I've already addressed that. As far as the message that Spanky left for Chip, I'm wondering if you'd care to evaluate it? It's already been dusted and chronicled. Thought you might deem something new or insightful. Another set of eyes can't hurt."

"Man, I'd love to help you guys," I insist. I bend my elbow and rest a clenched jaw on my palm against the butcher-block café table. Staring into space, gears and dials tumble in my head as I envision a potential breakthrough in the case from my interpretation of the handwriting results. I can't wait to tear home and proceed analyzing. According to my mentor, M. N. Bunker: "Writing is more than a mechanical operation; it is a process of putting on paper a picture of the way you think."

Lord, what is this lunatic thinking?

CHAPTER 36

I hustle home and hoof to the office. After burrowing through my desk drawers, I dig out a copy of *Encyclopedic Dictionary for Graphoanalysis*, twenty course instruction manuals, two basic-traits volumes, and a plastic gauge resembling a protractor -- to calculate expressiveness.

I swivel toward my Dell Inspiron and begin notating. Aware that neither gender nor age can be determined in handwriting samples, I concentrate on "brain writing" -- the letters formed by mental directives. Even people without hands, who scrawl with teeth or toes, will reveal their own persona.

The first step is to determine the emotional responsiveness as indicated in angle measurements of one-hundred consecutive upstrokes. I will ascertain the true identity, in this case, Spanky, a.k.a. Father Paul.

Objectiveness rules when a vertical incline is displayed. The writer will look before leaping -- exhibiting poise and cool judgment. Frequently these individuals come off as self-centered and egotistical. Regardless, the further the slant banks left, the more certainty the scripter will conceal his or her genuine feelings, despite external signs. Trust me, if you see a girl from this category crying -- it's strictly for effect only.

Conversely, the right-pitch penman and those registering deeper degrees in that direction, will outwardly respond readily to their circumstances.

Emotions are the basis of all human relations. Once you know the author of the handwriting through analysis, you know how he or she will react in daily life.

M's and n's indicate thought processes, while circle letters and *e's* are portholes to everyday living. Tall loops establish abstract thinking; d's and t's monitor pride and dignity, in beliefs and dress. Backward-stoke tendencies must be accounted for too -- signifying the possibility of withdrawal in the personality.

Also I will scrutinize for signs to identify: self-esteem, drive, enthusiasm, temper, fears, defenses and stubbornness.

Finally, I will inspect for light or heavy script to confirm emotional intensity. Weighty writers who demonstrate dark, thick lines as opposed to thin, airy ones, tend to hang on to feelings, soaking up experiences like a loofa. These experiences eventually foster permanent changes in one's makeup.

Often times these writers present a strong development of the senses, as well as a fondness for color -- desiring to be surrounded by deep shades. This group also enjoys feasting on rich foods, and chillin' with robust tones. Chefs, politicians, authors, actors, and musicians cram the category. This crowd -- the pleasure-seekers -- features many of my friends and relatives. Rock on!

In addition, these guys and gals share another common denominator: a strong desire for sex.

CHAPTER 37

Contemplating the outcome of my handwriting assessment, I wince when my cell sings.

"Frankie. Thought I was gonna call *you*?"

Despite the fact he has the patience of a spider monkey, even now I practically wet myself visualizing his firm tush and the outline of his bulge in tight blue jeans.

"Maria, Maria, O Sole Mia," he croons.

I acknowledge his playful banter from high school, replying in-kind: "Frankie, Frankie, bo Brankie, Banana fanna fo Rankie..."

"There you are, you got your groove on, girl. Ready to step out and boogie?"

"For real? Dude, I learned the hard way -- you got lyin' eyes and cheatin' feet. *And,* you can't control your hands neither. Ergo, I'm gonna take a pass."

I slouch back in a green padded desk chair and symbolically pat myself on the back. Even though I mouth, *no, no,* my pinky parts murmur, *yes, please.*

* * *

The first time I met Frankie -- my sixth sense in apparel prompts me -- he sported an azure blue striped oxford shirt, sleeves rolled, snug Levi's, and loafers with no socks. Yummy.

I was outfitted in standard parochial dress code -- a burgundy-plaid jumper with a white Peter-Pan-collar blouse. The instant class was dismissed, I paired the uniform with a black lace crop top, an accessory detail to sex up the after-hours school attire. Beneath the dress, fulfilling a dare from best bud LuAnne to *go commando,* the breeze wafted over my bare bum. Call me a basket of crazy. Must admit my sensations were exponentially empowered while my resistance was radically reduced while *au naturale.*

"Hanky-panky, puddin' and pie, kiss the girls and make them cry." I taunt.

"Thank you, Maria. I'm totally down with the 'hanky-panky' challenge. But, let's be clear. Are you truly game? Or are you just a *tease?*"

"Ouch! I've come a long way, baby. I'll accept your invite, but, for munchies only -- no *Sex in the City,* like days gone by."

"Ha, ha. Like that's all I'm after. Machinations to get near your *hoo ha!* Don't you recall lady, I'm a leg man? Butts and boobs are good, but I go for the gams every time."

"Sure you do. Cuz all guys flock to strip clubs for the *legs,* right? If memory serves me, recently you and brother Dante were crowned captains of industry with a new venture -- Paradise Playground -- the adult site just south of the West Des Moines city limits."

"Play nice, Maria. It's a legitimate enterprise. After the topless car wash tanked, Dad continues to feel we have something to offer men looking for good, clean fun."

"No doubt, Frankie, but don't guys need the wash *after* leaving your new venue?"

"Time out, doll. I'm gonna take a leap of faith and assume you're not interested in dinner or dancing. What say lunch, tomorrow?"

"Whatever;" I waver. "Text me the when and where. I'll think about it."

* * *

Tonight at lights out, I will include an extra decade of the Rosary to keep impure thoughts at bay.
Who am I kidding?

CHAPTER 38

I banish Frankie from my brain. Time to dive into preparing a narrative for Rocco, based on Spanky's writing specimen.

* * *

Here's what I have determined:

The guy has major problems. Even though he appears spirited and confident, he generally controls his emotions and most often conceals them for fear of criticism.

Our greatest need is to be loved and valued. Situations and events experienced by Spanky within his family, have completely conditioned his character. This conditioning clearly prevented his personality from developing normally. He carries the effects of these struggles with him today and they are at the root of his depraved behavior.

He has been deeply hurt, suffering a great deal; the consequence is an extremely strong emotional skepticism. His attitude toward love would be to eliminate it from life, although he attaches much importance to it. He is incapable of loving anyone -- including himself.

Signs of self-defensiveness are evident, traced to Spanky's reaction to disappointment. He derives satisfaction from staying within his own world, with no desire to emerge from his shell. This inner sphere provides protection from others, though he will step out of his safety zone, but, only when he is in charge.

He possesses an intuitive intelligence, fueled by a complimentary sensitivity. He constantly devours information and small details, which ultimately are processed by his intuition. Later, it appears in ways that no one could predict -- helping him resolve problems or follow a new course of action.

Along with traits of deceit, impatience and nonconformity, Spanky exhibits vanity -- exaggerated pride with an exceptionally high regard for self, bordering on narcissism. Only when Spanky's best interests are at heart, will he exert himself.

Summed up: Spanky is a bad, sad, seed. In his defense -- he comes by it honestly. Only God knows what this kid was dealt in childhood.

Initially, he will satisfy his cravings. Secondly, he will always protect himself when doing so.

I would assume he has assaulted many times before, and with further investigation, he may be exposed as a serial rapist. His attacks on women are more about control and violence, rather than sexual gratification.

He relies on his instincts, instead of rational, logical analysis. His easy-going smiling façade may open doors: his dark side, and his corrupt conduct, however, will repeatedly slam them shut.

* * *

Holy shit, I feel drained after Spanky's evaluation. I meander to my boudoir and collapse onto the pillow-topped bed. I snuggle up to a plush, white teddy-bear, a Valentine's Day gift.

Thank you Lord, for exemplary parents and a happy childhood.

CHAPTER 39

After relishing a twenty-minute cat-nap, I rouse to a text from Chip: *"Headin' to Nataliya's to study for a Latin test, Momma. Probably won't be home until 10...ish. Love you."*

Funny, thinking about my son I remember the *Mother Goose* nursery rhyme, "This Little Piggy Went to Market," that I frequently repeated to him as a child, counting on his fingers, wriggling his toes:

Hic parvus porcus venit in forum.

Hic parvus porcus remansit in domi.

Hic parvus porcus habuit carnes bovines assus.

Hic parvuc porcus non habuit.

Hic parvus porcus exclamavit oui oui; porci dixerant oink, oink.

I learned the poem on the first day of 9th grade Latin class. God knows it's like 500 years old. Hmm, might be the only thing I learned, other than the liturgy for celebrating Mass.

Clancy calls.

"Hey, sweet cheeks, what ya doin'?" he bellows.

"Just hopin' I'd hear from you, hoser. Did you put out your fire?"

Clancy had dumped me to extinguish a strip-mall blaze in Clive last night.

"Sort of. But I've got something here in my pants aging for you."

What a geek; then a pulsing begins.

"So, dude, bring it on."

* * *

Sex is like a sugar addiction -- the more you get, the more you want.

Wireless connections and web cams are ideal for long-distance stimulation. Even so, you can't beat the real thing -- touching and being touched, by someone else, I mean.

Peppermint gloss slathered over lips, transferred to my partner, then conveyed back to my mouth, tongue, nipples ....Tangy, tasty, and titillating, with a tiny sting. When dry, wet wand and reapply.

* * *

"Want me to pick up sushi and a Redbox title? I heard the guys at the station talking up, *The Crypt*."

"Okay, Kemo Sabe. Hurry though, I'm starving. Except, I'm not familiar with that film. Sounds scary. What's it about?"

"It's a thriller with six young thieves who rob jewelry from graves in catacombs beneath a Midwestern town. Supposedly the tombs are guarded by some strange bedfellows."

"Uh, these guys don't get caught in the tunnels, do they, Clancy? I'm soooooo claustrophobic."

"Maria, might be a cuddling opportunity," he hints. "Capiche?"

I roll my eyes. Oh, baby, I certainly *do* understand.

CHAPTER 40

I email Spanky's writing results to Rocco, though I cross my fingers that he won't want to discuss the details tonight.

After a two-minute shower, I sweep a comb through golden locks, dab on carbon-black mascara, cherry lipstick and Chloe Eau De Parfum, before stepping into a white cotton sleeveless sundress. The sweetheart neckline accentuates my décolleté with its cinched bodice and fitted shelf-bra -- for easy access. The full skirt flaunts appliqued florae in muted pastels along the hemline.

I don a risqué red-shimmer thong panty -- in case Clancy concocts his way to the jackpot. Ooh la la!

Ring, ring, ring. Christ, is there no solitude in this world anymore?

"Yes, Rocco, calling about my assessment?" I figure he has questions regarding Spanky's profile.

"Negatory, Maria, I'll check back with you on that score. I've got something else cookin'. Did I catch you at a good time?"

"Not exactly, boss, I'm heading out soon." Liar, liar, pants on fire. Of course I will regret this fib at some point in the near future. I never could lie well; I always get caught.

"Cool. I'll make it fast then. We're working a new development concerning the staff at St. Mark's Elementary," he shares. "Didn't Chip go there for grade school?"

"Actually we moved from the south side the year Chip turned five. He was registered at St. Mark's for kindergarten only, attended St. Bernard's for first through eighth grade, prior to Immaculate Mary. What's the fuss, Rocco?"

"Seems a former student, now a twenty-nine-year-old attorney, pummeled a retired priest at his residence this morning. The lawyer apparently recognized the padre when he literally bumped into him at the court house. He followed him home -- to a property that houses clergy accused of sexual indiscretions. The meeting evidently triggers a reckless response from the young man, with flashbacks of alleged molestations by this preacher some twenty years earlier."

I take a second to wrap my head around the twisted, convoluted scenario. "I think I get it. The lawyer's horrific memories come flooding back, after seeing the priest. Then, sensing danger, he freaks out and pounds the cleric for past transgressions."

"Pretty much, Maria. Presumably the statute of limitations has long since expired for filing criminal charges, so without warning the young guy takes the law into his own hands and goes ballistic on Fr. Philip Carney, packing a punch that launches him to the emergency room. He's awaiting surgery."

"That's harsh, though feasibly justified."

"Hell, yeah!" Rocco cries out. "The cleric was a total tool. Hey, wondered if you or Chip had any knowledge of past misconduct by the staff at St. Mark's?"

"I certainly don't; and it's doubtful that Chip had much contact with the parish pastor then, assuming it's the same douche you're referring to now. Not like he was an altar boy with access to the sacristy." Cognizant of Rocco's affinity for nailing creeps to the cross, I speculate, "Are you personally conducting the investigation in this case?"

"Touch base with you later, cuz." He disconnects.

Hmm, why had Rocco dissed me so, and not answered my question? Bad day?

* * *

I pray for every child who has been abused in the Church for possibly millenniums, while *the powers that be* turned a blind eye. Years of Catholic hierarchy -- Bishops, Archbishops, Cardinals, and Monsignors, who knows, even Popes -- relocating pedophile priests, instead of reporting them.

I'm reminded: (*Romans 3:23) "For all have sinned..."*

CHAPTER 41

I tap in brother Nick's cell number to discuss arrangements for supper next week.

"Great then," Nick adds, "we'll expect you Sunday afternoon at 4:00, assuming Chip doesn't have a soccer match or a previous commitment with his girlfriend. Now, Maria, how's life treating you?" he probes. "And my nephew, is he staying in line?"

"I'm good. As far as Chip, he seems to be enjoying the start of senior year. No worries."

I hesitate to share particulars, including news of our caper with Rocco and the Des Moines Police. My brother wouldn't approve, and the deal is *complicated*. Besides, I'm not actively pursuing criticism these days.

"Excellent. See you soon," Nick signs off.

* * *

The moments are few and fleeting, so I draw a breath of relief when Clancy finally sets foot inside.

"Bonjour," I spout. Happy to see you -- I'm famished."

"Maria, I'm hungry too," he confesses, as his gaze gloms on my chest.

Immediately he releases the brown paper bags containing plastic trays of sushi, ditches the DVD, and draws me into his arms. After a prolonged erotic smooch with tongues tangling, he buries his face between my breasts in a valley of no return. My bosom literally pops out of the wire confines, which doesn't appear to be a problem for either of us.

His right hand slithers up my leg, nuzzling in *the zone*. I recognize the resolve in his eyes -- a man on a mission. Whatever he's after, it's a done deal. He pins me against the double entry doors and drops down on his knees. Probably not a proposal, nor a prayer. Urgently he stretches my panty aside, ultimately snatching up *the prize*. I melt into a hot mess.

"Clancy, I think I hear the garage door. It must be Chip!"

Panic sets in. Pronto, I adjust my dress and stuff my boobs back into the bustier. Sure enough, a millisecond later, Chip descends upon us.

"Dude," Chip calls out, extending his arm toward Clancy. "Hey, Mom, what up?"

"Honey, you're home earlier than I expected," I sputter, aiming to maintain composure. Busted. No way Chip didn't eyeball Clancy's *stiffy*.

After the guys shake hands, we angle our way toward the kitchen.

"Sorry to intrude, Mom. Nataliya and Lily were required to attend a *Step Sisters* meeting at the last minute. Guess the drill team has advanced again. Ergo -- road trip to Chicago for 'Nationals'."

"Impressive," I add. "The corps has won every championship award conceivable in the past sixty years. Also, they're touted as 'The Nation's Finest Drill Team.' They were even invited to march in President Kennedy's Inaugural Parade in '61, but the nuns would have none of it. Too much temptation, I guess."

"My my, Maria, you're certainly dialed in on this subject. Did you always want to be a Stepper?"

"Something like that," I reply. My older sister Jenny had been a certified card-carrying member of the prestigious group, when she was enrolled at Immaculate Mary. Hence, I have first hand knowledge as to the amount of time and dedication necessary to yield the experience.

"Good to know Lily is bouncing back," I direct toward Chip.

He purses his lips, so I sense he wants me to deep-six the topic.

"Chip, I brought along sushi from The Mai Tai around the corner. There's plenty for all of us," Clancy offers.

"No thanks, guys. I'm gonna head up to my room to study for Latin. Good to see you, Clancy. He leans over the counter and pecks me on the cheek. "See you in the morning, Mom. *Valete,*" he announces, waving.

"Huh?" Clancy mutters, confused.

"*Farewell,* in Latin."

Chip is no sooner out of sight, when Clancy resumes his sensual assault, this time letting his fingers do the walking.

"Are you insane?" I giggle, not really resisting, though I smack his paws. "I swear, you're like a dog in heat."

"That's a given, Maria, you bring out the beast in me," Clancy insists. "Though, honestly babe, I'm way more of a pussycat, than a pooch."

Mew, mew.

CHAPTER 42

My ears rally to a ringing cell, long before my eyes can focus. The clock, positioned on a rattan nightstand, flashes 4:35 a.m. I brace for the outcome: exceptional news -- or death. Nothing in between at this hour.

"Pretty early, Rocco. Must be important." He's notorious for disturbing sleep and sex -- though not necessarily in that order. I scope my memory foam mattress, then peer beneath the covers for a partner. I'm alone.

"I apologize, girl, but I got to count my lucky stars -- thank the Lord above before I burst. Besides, you're the only other goofball I know up at this hour. Anyway, I have an update regarding Spanky, our pervert fake-priest. We've been collecting data and it just so happens he's scammed his way in and out of several similar situations. We originally were hung up, cuz the scumbag is so sketchy -- impersonating other occupations with different identities. The guy's a pig, what can I say. The District Attorney is pretty confident we can convict him with an extended-stay in the slammer."

"Without a doubt." I agree. "Though I feel compassion for his lot in life. If we would all start out even, the stakes would be fair. But, we don't. So, none of us can truly appreciate another's journey, including the obstacles and desperate revisions along the way." Wow, I really sound preachy.

"Boo hoo. Tough shit, Maria, no sympathy here. Granted, he's damaged; who isn't? And, he has no moral compass. If he did, he'd probably direct it due south toward a woman's *vagaygay*," cries Rocco.

"Seriously, you're playing the Oprah card? Come on. I think you're goin' soft on me."

"Don't ever say that!"

"Is that the worst thing a guy can hear?" I heckle.

"Close, but no cigar. The four most frightening words for a man: *Is it in yet?*"

"Time out, cuz. I haven't even had my coffee yet. Besides, I heard the most dreaded words a guy can hear from his partner is: *I've been thinking...*"

"Back on track, lassie. I also called to tell you, that after a year, we're following a reputable lead regarding Joey Gannon. His mom, Nora claims her son appeared last night at 11:45 p.m. at their family home in West Des Moines. Oh, yeah, while her husband, Judd was away at an agriculture convention."

"Really," I gasp, "like an apparition *appeared* or a down-to-earth flesh-and-blood visit?" I know the lady well, and even though barbs have been hurled against her sanity, she's a straight shooter in my eyes. I trust her.

"Maria, supposedly the kid showed up, chugged a Pepsi, before suddenly shoving off to who knows where. I'm not buyin' it. I think she's a whack-job."

"Oh, ye of little faith, Rocco. At any rate, what did he say? Is he free to come home? Is he no longer considered abducted or a run-away?"

"That's the thing. No one else was privy to the encounter. Consequently, the report is unsubstantiated -- we can't confirm the sighting."

"The sighting? Christ, he's not a UFO or an alien! He's a missing kid and we want him tucked in his own bed tonight."

"I'm workin' on it. By the way, heads up. I'm undergoing a review by Internal Affairs vis-à-vis my involvement with the Timmoms -- Lily's parents. My lieutenant reported me for insubordination, pursuant to my attitude. Sorry if I came off pissy last night. No disrespect."

"We're all good, Rocco."

* * *

A sense of calm washes over me after Rocco's newsflash and his apology. Regarding Nora, well, naïve or not, my perception is that she's on solid ground. I know her as a focused, confident, and compelling woman. She and her hubby didn't summon the spotlight -- their son's disappearance did that for them. "But for the grace of God go I." I wouldn't trade places for the world.

I hop up and pad to the kitchen to surprise Chip with his favorite breakfast -- crepes. I readily rustle up fixings for Grammy's renowned recipe of 3-2-1: three eggs, two cups milk and one cup flour, combined with salt, sugar, oil, and a smidge of vanilla extract. As soon as the grease dances in the fry pan, I ladle in a small portion of batter and spread it to the edge by tilting the skillet.

At the same time, I measure one cup sugar and a half cup water into a saucepan. I switch on the flame and simmer the ingredients after spiking with a capful of maple flavoring and a hunk of butter. Next, I flip the thin flapjack and repeat the cooking process a few more times. I pull out ceramic dishes and silverware, and arrange the nummies on two plates. Finally, I sift powdered sugar over the rolled crepes, dollop with butter, before garnishing with fresh strawberries and scalding copper-colored syrup. Bon appetite!

"Mom, what smells so good?" Chip drifts downstairs and parks himself on a barstool. "Grammy's famous pancakes? And it's not even my birthday. What happened? Did we win the lottery?"

"No, dear, you'd have to play the lottery. But, I'm feelin' some good vibrations."

At once the red Cuisinart toaster oven *dings*, without benefit of toast. The ghosts of Christmas past are upon us.

Our eyes meet; we laugh, while we scrape our plates clean.

CHAPTER 43

Chip shoves aside his Fiestaware, and after grasping a glass of milk he turns to face me at the counter. "Want to run something by you, Mom."

"Absolutely," I urge. "What's up?"

"This is weird," he begins, "but, even though I adore Nataliya, I really dig Lily." He stares at the ceiling, propping his right elbow on the granite, running his hand roughly over his head in a scratching fashion.

"Guess what? You can be friends with both girls."

"Nah," he continues, "I kinda wanna be *more* than friends."

Hmm, the damsel dilemma -- and such a young pup. "Okay, tell me about it. What's the attraction?"

"Well, it's hard to explain, Mom. One thing is the way Lily flips her long black hair -- I wanna run my hands through it. And when she smiles, she keeps her lips pinched together, except her eyes sparkle."

Damn, he's got it bad. Reminds me of *The Godfather* when Michael, after beholding the lovely Apollonia for the first time, is struck by "the Thunderbolt" -- a powerful, nearly perilous yearning.

"Oh, yeah, I get that. Pure physical appeal."

"No, not totally. I was thinking because of Lily's abduction and assault, I relate to her. You know, misery loves company. Maybe due to Dad's death, I feel a connection with her – I can be myself. Sounds strange, but it could be pain that binds us."

Mercy, the wisdom of Job. At seventeen I was dodging chores and choreographing dance moves for Friday night mixers. Who is this kid? Obviously his experience with Michael's passing last year continues to haunt him and weighs heavily on his heart. He's searching for someone to confide in, someone to share the grief.

"Chip, that's quite insightful, though it's not unusual for kindred spirits to align. Heads up; with Lily's recent rape looming, she's probably overwhelmed and particularly vulnerable now. You need to be exceptionally considerate and understanding.

Insightful also on my part for registering that Chip failed to mention Lily's current college boyfriend, Tyler. Also, I wonder how Chip would feel if he jilted Nataliya. *The thought plickens.*

Each of us has suffered traumatic events: the death of a loved one, a divorce, illness or injury, loss of a job. The combination of these challenges and the way we cope with them, comprise our ever-changing personalities -- notably apparent in handwriting variances.

I relax back till my shoulders rest on the stool spindles. My son shuffles off to school. Imploring guidance for all, I murmur:

> *All for Thee my Jesus,*
> *my Jesus, all for Thee,*
> *in union with the intentions*
> *of Thy most Sacred Heart.*

* * *

I had scheduled an appointment with Jason, my hottie general contractor, for 9:00 a.m. to rectify repair costs at the condo remodel. After assembling the folder labeled *2327,* I clutch my cell, business checkbook, and a thermos of Starbuck's before heading out. I no sooner fasten into the British racing green Z3, when the Bluetooth buzzes.

My eyes flash toward the radio tuner, acknowledging Rocco as the caller. I recall Nate's warning to Andy Sacks in *The Devil Wears Prada*: "The person whose calls you always take? That's the relationship you're in." Whatever.

"Maria, are you sitting down?"

CHAPTER 44

"Dude, I'm in the car. I'm positive I'm sitting down. What's the news notice?"

"Maria," blares Rocco, "Spanky Collier, aka Fr. Paul is *dead!*"

"What the hell!" I shriek. "Did the prick poke his pecker somewhere it didn't belong?"

"You could say that. When he was out on bail, Collier hopped a Greyhound to Leon, some sixty-five miles south of here. He was an infamous manipulator, so, it was no surprise when he conned his way into a random family reunion -- donning clerical clothing with a white tab collar. He lured a curvy fourteen-year-old girl inside a nearby timber cattle barn. After anesthetizing her with chloroform and stripping her clean to the waist, he molested her. Unbeknownst to him, the teen's father had tailed the pair to the wooden structure. Trust me; Spanky's *woody* came tumblin' down."

"Whoa, Rocco, *how* did his 'woody' come down?"

"Walloped, with a hatchet. A gory mess, I hear. It hurts like hell to even imagine."

"*Eew!* Guess he bled to death?"

"Yep, the bloke expired from blood loss. Too bad he croaked so fast. Personally I would have preferred he suffer more, like his conquests. It took a special kind of stupid to be Spanky; I won't miss him."

"Will the dad be charged with murder or manslaughter?" I've often pondered if interfering in the rape of a child would be justifiable self defense of a minor.

"I'll go out on a limb and predict that any rational judge will dismiss the case. Otherwise, if it goes to trial, a jury will certainly acquit," Rocco reasons.

"What a relief for Lily. There must be some solace in *not* facing one's perpetrator across a court room. And consolation in moving on and hopefully leaving her encounter with Spanky in the dust."

Of course I know the severity of the offenses she endured -- kidnapping, assault, rape -- will forever alter her life and personality. Shit, she could be pregnant. Nevertheless, what had German philosopher, Nietzsche said? "That which doesn't kill us, makes us stronger"...or has the potential to.

* * *

As I approach the renovation property, my view flies toward Jason. He stands with legs crossed, propped against his spotless Mocha Metallic Chevy Silverado. His pose, beside his steel steed -- nostalgic, as I recollect a TV commercial from the '70s, with the rugged robust Marlboro Man, sans white Stetson.

He lifts his hand *howdy*, extinguishing a cigarette butt with the heel of his CAT work boot. He bends down and picks up the spent smoke remains and tucks them in his front denim pocket.

I think: oh baby, don't go burnin' your privates!

"Hey, there," he stares, running his baby blues from my head to my peds, then up again. I feel consumed by his eyes.

Chills run through me. I suspect it's gonna be hard to concentrate this morning. Must be true that women reach our sexual peak in our forties. Otherwise I'm at a loss for words -- or excuses.

"Jason, thanks for meeting me. Let's go inside and settle up." Or, *saddle up?*

He unlocks the building with the master key, then holds the door for me. We reach Unit #18, on the second floor, where he opens that door too. I'm a sucker for chivalry.

"Maria, I hope to be squared away with this project in a week or two. Thanks for the check and for hiring me. Please let me know if I can be of assistance in the future."

Um, yeah, I can be assisted, I fantasize.

"You're welcome, Jason. Leave me some business cards, I'll send you referrals if I get the chance."

"I appreciate it," he nods.

* * *

Here's the thing: hip hooray for tomfoolery. Distractions from life with characters like Frankie, Clancy, and Jason, bode well for a sound mind. To provide balance, optimism is required to break reality's back. What better way than with eye candy and bad boys?

I split, eager for time to absorb the morning. I make a b-line to St. Joseph's to meditate on the Stations of the Cross, a collection of fourteen artistic depictions of the Passion and death of Our Lord. Commonly observed during Lent -- a six-week span preceding Easter -- the Stations have provided definition in an age of injustice. I begin a rotation through the church, surrounded by flickering candle-light, panes of stained glass, and a veil of Monastery incense. As I visualize aspiring Lily, tears trail down my cheeks.

I whisper: *Please Lord, forgive motherfucker Spanky and close this chapter.*

CHAPTER 45

I had dialed down the volume on my cell inside church, but the phone continues to vibrate feverishly. Really? Is there no peace? My bad; I should have ditched the damn thing in the car. My eyes slide into slits as I peek down at the recognizable number. I dart outdoors to answer.

"Hello?"

"Ms. Magliani, this is Monsignor Macy from Immaculate Mary. *Maria, 'we have a problem'.*"

A twinge of terror strikes me and I quiver. I flop down onto a wrought-iron bench beside a gurgling fountain near the entrance. That declaration prompts memories of the Apollo 13 lunar mission when an explosion sparked a power malfunction, with the risk of crippling the craft and its crew in space forever.

"What's wrong, Father? Is Chip alright?"

"He's fine; he's here in the office with me now. However," he pauses, "we've made a dismal discovery."

"Okay," Lord, cut to the chase, I beg silently.

The priest resumes. "When the girls' lacrosse team was running laps, their path clipped the student parking lot where Chip's Honda was positioned in his designated stall. The coach detected a red, gooey substance oozing from the trunk, onto the bumper, ultimately pooling on the concrete."

I clear my throat. "I'm confused, Father, are you implying that Chip's car is leaking *blood?*" When I envision the maroon-colored sticky sludge, my anxiety ramps up, but I try my best to remain calm for clarity.

"At this time we have summoned the police, and cannot comment further on our discovery. Nevertheless Maria, it's mandatory we receive your permission to question your son, since he is under eighteen years old. Are you agreeable?"

Pssst. Note to self: Daddy said to deny everything at first -- you can always change your mind later, when you actually have the facts.

"No, Father, I'm sorry. Please delay the interrogation until I reach school and visit with Chip first."

"That is your right, dear. See you shortly."

I sprint to the Beamner and blaze away -- destination: Immaculate Mary.

As I crank up an iHeartRadio station, my Bluetooth beeps in with a call from Clancy. "Good morning, sunshine. How's your day going?"

"All good." I wouldn't dare drown Clancy in details of my dysfunctional family -- you have to earn that thrill. Instead I dodge the truth a teeny. "Just cruising to meet Chip about a car glitch. Are you signed on for a twenty-four hour shift today?"

"Yes, ma'am. But I'm preoccupied dreaming about my forty-eight hours *off!* What are the chances we might hook-up then?"

"Like Ivory soap -- 99.44% pure."

He fires back, "As we speak, I'm picturing you, me, *and...*"

I punch the brakes to avoid a three-way collision!

"Hey there Don Juan, that sounds crude, rude, lewd and socially unacceptable! Besides, I don't share well -- particularly the love stick. Let's chuck that topic till you're off-duty."

Holy crap, I can only imagine Clancy's trifecta fancies. What would *Father* say? Or *my* father, for that matter. I peer into the rear-view mirror. Sure enough, my face is flushed.

"Maria, hope you're not offended…or embarrassed. You Catholic girls come late to the party and then leave early. Incidentally, are your cheeks pink?"

Where's he going with this? "Yeah, so?"

"Good girls *blush*."

CHAPTER 46

Rolling into the campus parking lot, I spot a hive
of activity. My attention drills toward a fleet of black-
and-whites with syncopated flickering light bars.
Trouble city. A Sheriff's deputy elevates an arm,
signaling me to pull over. Unfortunately I fail to
spot Rocco; I assumed he would be there for me to
run interference -- however, you know what happens
when you assume.

"Ms. Magliani," a distant voice emanates through
the air. I spin my head around like Linda Blair in
The Exorcist, and target Detective Sergeant Ryne

Wittry from a cadre of cops. He's one of my cousin's pals from the force. The thirty-something, tall robust redhead hustles over and acknowledges me with a wave. Funny, I thought we were more familiar. Then again I recount Rocco revealing that some officers *never* shake hands. Seemingly innocent situations can escalate quickly when combined with angry, fearful, or chemically-impaired individuals, eventually ratcheting to life-or-death status. Hence, most policemen and women, ensure that their hands are weapon-ready at all times.

"Det. Wittry," I lean forward, cup my fingers and whisper, "did you draw the short straw?" -- referring to his bad luck in drawing me.

"No, no. Det. Randazzo is busy assisting on a break in a cold case. He sends his regards."

"Great." A pang pierces my core. Bummer, now I have to fly solo for the interrogation.

"Don't worry, girl," Ryne assures, lowering his tone, "I promised my buddy I'd see you through this. It's all good." He accentuates his words with a nod.

I spy forensics collecting DNA samples from the Honda compact. No doubt the specimens will be packed off to the lab in Ankeny for testing. In the past, positive identification results have required 5-10 days, or as long as six weeks for diagnosis. Hell, hair, blood, skin, whatever they ascertain, might end up belonging to a dog, a rabbit, or even a fucking raccoon squirreled away in the vehicle's booty. Nervously I dab perspiration from my brow. Damn hot flashes.

I'm escorted to the principal's office and united with my son.

* * *

Hours later after being grilled, we bound to the BMW. My eyes flutter as I survey Chip's auto: hoisted, suspended from a sling hook, and in the process of being hauled away by a prominent Des Moines towing service -- new meaning for me to roadside assistance. I fret as to the significance of the evidence that may lie within the trunk. And ultimately, will we be wrongfully accused or charged?

"Maria," Sgt Wittry shares, "we found articles of clothing in the Civic, and a tattered and torn Iowa Driver's License issued by the DOT a little over a year ago. Also, there is a source of blood, yet to be determined. Do you have any insights regarding our findings?"

Crap, with tension mounting, I hesitate before answering. I hate this cat-and-mouse game of assigning blame. In my defense, I didn't even drive that car, and certainly Chip is innocent of any wrongdoing.

"Well, it's likely that Chip would store and transport gym shorts and tee shirts for soccer practice in the rear compartment, so probably some of the threads and prints are his. As for the driver's license, I'm clueless -- though, maybe that's his too." My stomach does flips -- like Mexican jumping beans.

My cell sings, labeling Rocco on the other end.

"Dude, what is going on?" I blurt. "I'm in agony here."

"My God," he gasps, "You won't believe this."

CHAPTER 47

Fear grips me like a vice.

"Maria, the trace evidence -- the ripped Iowa Driver's License discovered in Chip's trunk -- was issued to Joey Gannon."

My composure breaks. Instantly I train my gaze toward my son, strapped in the passenger seat of my car. He sits with his mouth gaping -- the news bulletin penetrates his very soul too.

"What the fuck, Rocco? That's inconceivable. Joey was only twelve when he went missing a year ago. Don't you have to be fourteen to even apply for a driving permit?" I'm pulling out all stops -- diligent to disassociate Chip and me from the madness.

"You got that right, girl. We have yet to authenticate the card. We'll examine the paper, holograms and security overlay, probing for fraud. We'll also verify a few features -- the frayed photo, placement of the State seal, and the ink's sensitivity to ultraviolet lights. But come on, testing aside, I can't wrap my head around the possibility of the boy's body in your car."

Of course, I detect frustration in his voice. Big time. Weird, I remember the day Joey vanished. Immediately after visiting with his dad Judd Gannon, I had phoned Rocco and he practically chortled when I proposed the youngster may have been kidnapped. He and the police department insisted on waiting twenty-four hours before even filing a missing person's report. Rocco had reassured me: "I suspect the kid will be safely tucked in his bed by nightfall." My my, if only that were true.

"Cuz, I'm speechless." I recollect his mother, Nora, reiterating that she had spoken with him just days earlier. I ponder the possibility.

"Maria, I pray he surfaces soon -- breathing and in one piece. Maybe his momma wasn't zany after all. We put a rush on the DNA evidence, so I'll keep you apprised of any breakthroughs."

Rocco signs off; now I have to deal with my son.

"Mom, I dig you support me and believe I played no part in any scheme regarding Joe, but we gotta get to the bottom of this. Let's retrace our steps this morning." His eyes roll back like a slot machine. "When I hopped in the car to head out, I noticed nothing peculiar -- no apparent signs of vandalism or red seeping secretions from the rear. Therefore the foul play definitely took place after I arrived at school."

"Impressive, Sherlock. So, when was the last time you actually checked your cargo? You know, for textbooks, soccer garb, water bottles?'

'Yesterday,."

"Right. But remember Chip, the Honda doesn't include a lock assembly on the trunk itself; I always thought that was a flaw in the design. At any rate, to gain access to it you must either use the remote on the key or enter through the car, and then manually pull the release inside. Are you with me?"

I flash a look at Chip and discern a sheepish grin.

"Um, I'm sorry Mom. I might have forgotten to mention that I misplaced my keys. I'm using the spare set."

CHAPTER 48

"Nice job, Chip. So where the hell are your original keys?" I touch my temples with my hands, then begin kneading a hammering headache.

He shoots me a sideways stare. "Honestly? I generally leave them in the ignition overnight," he confesses, frowns and glances away.

I blow out a sigh, keenly aware that young and stupid are not mutually exclusive. "Awesome!"

"I was already running late this morning to meet up with classmates for an anatomy project, when I realized the keys were AWOL. I panicked, snagged the spare set in the kitchen cupboard and bounced."

"You know with them missing, it's possible that some thieves got access, not only to the car, but also to our house -- with the garage door opener?" A chill jogs up my spine as I imagine the worst.

"My bad," he acknowledges. "I just didn't give it much thought at the time. I figured I'd get it resolved after class today."

The Bluetooth rings. My eyes fly to the electronic display screen on the dashboard. Oh joy, it's Clancy. No way am I taking his call after his indecent proposal -- particularly with my son in the car. Besides, our lives are already spiraling out of control. I shrug my shoulders, turn to Chip and say, "I'm gonna let that go to voicemail. We need to stay on task."

"Mom, I'm sorry."

"Thank you; now let's get back to brainstorming. How could someone enter our garage -- and filch your keys?"

We arrive home, I zigzag up the coiled driveway and park. We continue dredging our wits for suspects.

"You know," Chip surmises, "when the cleaning ladies come every two weeks, they have to press in the garage code on the button pad to get inside. One of the girls -- or another employee at the company -- could have pinched the combination and helped themselves while we were away."

"Chip, good reasoning skills," I marvel. "Amazing Maids do have access, along of course, with my brother Nick and Aunt Jen. Obvious also is the number sequence that Grampie initially programmed -- #2222. I'm afraid it's not a very challenging cipher."

"Sure. Plus, possibly some random shuffled by, punched in a string of digits, and cracked our code. I heard about that scam on the *Iowa Today Show*. These creeps are like vultures; they just wait for a kid like me to screw up."

"Hey kiddo, kudos for taxing your noodle. But in the end, according to Holmes in *A Study in Scarlet*: 'There is nothing new under the sun. It has all been done before.' The question is: Why us? And, why now?"

CHAPTER 49

A telegraph tone alerts me to a new text. Chip bolts to the house as I divert my attention downward to my iPhone: *Babe, bought a bag of toys for us to try. Are you game? Just us.*

Holy cow, Clancy is like a dog on a bone. In particular, a terrier named Buddy.. In his defense, his handwriting professes persistence -- the spirit that will not admit defeat. Enduring perseverance is highly touted as a powerful success trait and he has it in spades. Admittedly I've always been attracted to tenacious macho men -- outwardly masculine, notably sensual, and damn pretty too. Why change now?

I've never fiddled with sex knick-knacks, though I am gifted with oodles of imagination. Most likely grape or watermelon or some other fruit-flavored lubricant will be among the goodies in Clancy's spicy sack, along with faux-fur handcuffs for ratified restraint, and scanty satin panties with a cotton-candy crotch. As I recall: *Erotic is when you use a feather; kinky... well, you know.*

Also enclosed might be blindfolds for all participants, and of course some form of a *neck massager* -- as attested by a Sharper Image employee who denied to *Sex and the City* Samantha, that the merchant ever carried a *vibrator.* Samantha's motivation for retuning the afore-mentioned item was because "it failed to get me off." Wow, we've come a long way, baby.

Perhaps another prime component of our fun-filled satchel will be an assortment of racy girl-guy and girl-on-girl DVDs. My son and friends tell me that women today are eager to experiment with their sexuality. Thus, the abundance of *all-girl* porn. And it goes without saying the material is an unquestionable turn-on for men. All in, I believe Clancy will have amassed the necessities for our own *Fifty Shades of Grey* tete-a-tete.

I was always curious as to the presence of gays and lesbians in high school. Granted the former, the gay guys, were amply represented in my all-female establishment of higher education, by the instructors of religion lessons -- the priests. Um, the latter, I just didn't know any. In retrospect, the girls who donned severe short hairstyles, devoid of makeup and jewelry, were suggestive of the lesbian ranks. Then again, no. Girly-girls also bat for the other team.

Enough. Regardless, Chip constantly scolds me if I inquire as to someone's sexual orientation. His advice: "Why would it matter? Don't judge. Ever."

These youngins do know *some* things.

CHAPTER 50

Buckled into the Beamer and texting contractor Jason about the Cedar Ridge reno job, I raise my chin in surprise when Chip thumps his knuckles on the driver-side window. "Good news, Mom," he crows, "Lily got her period!"

Wow, in my day, boys avoided this topic like VD -- at least in mixed company. Especially with a parent. I grin, grateful for a positive resolution.

"Thank God she's not pregnant. What a relief for Lily and her family."

"I'm stoked," he beams, radiating a smile from ear to ear. "Now she can move on with her life."

"Absolutely." I pause, then continue, "Am I to assume now she can move on with *you?*"

"Smooth, Mom." He cocks his head. "Though you know I haven't actually broken it off with Nataliya yet. I'm an ass."

Possibly dreading a reprimand from me, Chip squirms then shies away. I know he's no good at good-byes. Expressly with unexpected farewells. I put an arm out, wrapping it around his waist. "You'll do the right thing."

"Sure. But I'm hoping Nataliya gets the hint and blows me off first." He squints. "I mean, uh, you know...dumps me."

"I get it." We trot to the house. Chip shoves off to his room, while I brew a mug of French vanilla java. I settle in the den, sprawling upon a blonde bamboo lounger with a red, white and blue afghan that Grammie crocheted. My eyelids melt down as daylight streaks mesmerize me.

* * *

Mental notes of young lust, oops, I mean young *love*, drift across my noggin...and other parts. Parked with a boy on Lookout Ledge at the Des Moines Airport, hypnotized by flashing blue lights that border the taxiway, I reminisce about hormone-riddled adolescent couples groping for God's creation of beauty, in each other.

Not only did the sight of your sweetheart stir your insides, but even his scent sent nerve endings vibrating in all the right places. The stroke of his fingers in the palm of your hand; the swell of your breasts after his supple caress; open-mouth kisses awaiting tongue touching tongue...ah, the dalliance of foreplay.

* * *

Poof, abruptly my romantic dream vanishes when I'm disturbed by a voicemail from Rocco. Flushed, I play back his message: *"Maria, I've got news about Joey Gannon."*

CHAPTER 51

Unaware of Joey's fate -- whether he's alive or forever asleep, the Westminster door chimes peal and disturb my thoughts. I peep out through the sidelight window, flanking the oak double-door entry, and spy Frankie. Crap! Who invited *him?*

"Mom," Chip hollers from upstairs, "someone's here."

I dab my face with a sleeve, rake fingers through my hair, pan my appearance -- pulling and tugging garments into place -- then lob the door open. "Hey there, stranger."

Concealing my genuine elation, I assess, and at the same time absorb every square inch of Frankie's fine frame. My eyes soar first to ground level, prior to scanning up *s-l-o-w-l-y*. I might have paused momentarily at midpoint. Hey, no harm in a girl looking. He flaunts familiar signature lines: luxurious Italian Ferragamo loafers, Michael Kors charcoal skinny jeans, and a Ted Baker moss-green fitted sport coat, paired with a Ben Sherman paisley-print shirt. Damn, the man broadcasts style. Even his argyle socks got swag.

"Maria," he interjects, "I'm sorry to come by without calling first, but I had business in the area and spotted your ride in the drive. Hoping we might have lunch and catch up." Immediately he sashays nearer to me, stationing his hands on my waist, and cranes his neck in for a smacker.

What a fibber. The Frankie I know is never sorry about anything, especially if there is a prize to be gained. Even so, once I ingest the sweet essence of *Polo* cologne, my knees cave -- along with my resistance -- and I decide not to dodge the smooch. Obviously Frankie is experiencing an intense arousal also.

"Sounds like a plan, but I promised to meet with Rocco at the precinct." Although my schedule is not fixed, I prefer keeping my options open. *Always say 'no' to everything at first,* Daddy imparted, *you can change your mind later.* After gazing into Frankie's chocolate eyes and gushing a tiny, I resume, "I'm pretty much supposed to be tied up all day. We're collaborating on a venture, and we just had a break in the case."

Instantly I envision Frankie picturing me tied up*!* Instead, he frowns before shrugging it off. "No worries. I'm satisfied to just hang for a few," as he nestles closer.

Yeah, like that's gonna happen -- simply hang. Maybe hang lip, *kiss kiss,* or possibly hang on for dear life -- referring to naughty bits bumping in the night with Frankie in years past. Fully aware of his typical peppered banter, carnal wisecracks, and the ultimate outcome, I caution, "Heads up, player; we're not alone. Chip is upstairs." I tilt my eyes and head up toward the ceiling.

'Hey, Maria, I'd love to see the little guy. It's been awhile."

"Clearly, because the guy's not all that little anymore. He's sprung up five or six inches this year alone."

Frankie shakes his head and chortles. "How sad. A measly five or six inches? And, an Italian boy."

"*You* are a dirt bag!"

CHAPTER 52

Before Frankie and I can exchange...whatever, my cousin calls. I wink at Frankie, alerting him to a brief delay.

"Okay Rocco, what's the word?" Soon I sense the hackles on the back of my neck stand on end. I cup a hand around my mouth, fearful of his announcement.

"Well Maria, Joe Gannon is alive," concern registering in his voice. "The kid has been an unwilling member of a degenerate sex ring; but, he'll survive."

"What? Is he injured? How'd you find him?" Uncontrollably I spew a litany of questions. Then my gaze flits toward a bewildered Frankie, perhaps sorely aware that his rising prominence now has a diminished chance of *getting any.*

"For the past year Joe and several other boys were held against their will. Recently we rescued them near Omaha, and also apprehended many of their abductors. I would say yes, he's injured, though not with an observable wound. His blank stare, emptiness in his eyes, probably mask plenty of pain."

"Mercy, will these kids ever lead ordinary lives again?" Between Lily's and Joey's encounters, I'm appalled at the decadence in the world.

"I'm hopeful they will, yet sometimes this method of misery doesn't manifest in a timely or expected manner. I've seen abuse, particularly when young girls have been savagely beaten, leaving them mentally and emotionally devastated from mistreatment. The longer one remains in a depraved environment, the less likely a total healing process."

My skin shivers. Unwittingly I find myself nodding, even though my naiveté and lack of sophistication prevents me from fully understanding the depth of damage done. Despite my limitations, parenthood has provided me with an innate appreciation of life's fuck-ups. I admire my Rocco; all the same,

I speculate how he can sleep at night after daily exposure to life's most malevolent moments.

"Which is it then, Rocco: did you receive a tip on Joe's location, or did he escape?"

"Both."

CHAPTER 53

"Huh? How can that be?"

"Maria, give me an hour, I'll head your way. I'll explain everything then."

Rocco clicks *off*. Frankie turns *on*. He scooches a skosh closer when I drop down on a pleated blue velvet settee in the foyer. Even after being privy to breaking news regarding Joey, the man has no regard for anyone else - he's a bona fide narcissist.

"Maria, do me a solid," as he envelops me with stove-piped biceps tattooed with *BORN TOUGH* on one arm and a set of *angel wings* on the other, "let's jet out to my car and continue our conversation."

"Right, like we can't talk here?"

"I don't want to annoy Chip." He brushes a hand across my tatas, in pursuit of my hair, or shoulder, or something. "Can you still tie a cherry stem in a knot with your tongue?"

"What's on your mind, Frankie? Is it that time of the month?" Routinely in the past, he'd stop in to shoot the breeze; we'd go for a spin and eventually hook up for a quickie. "You know I'm seeing Clancy now, so there's no messing around with you. One guy at a time, buddy."

"Bullshit!" he howls. "Do you always have to play by the rules, Maria? You good girls are *no* fun."

With that, he strokes my face and splits.

* * *

"Well," Rocco resumes, "remember when we discovered Joe's DNA and partial driver's permit in Chip's trunk?"

"Of course; go on."

"Uh...we planted them."

"Seriously? And the blood?"

"Yep, that too. Recently our agency was approached by an informant, a lad in his early twenties who'd spent six years imprisoned in a 'sex den' --equipped with caves, tunnels, and a dungeon where abductees were imprisoned, all enshrouded on a remote ranch less than a hundred and thirty miles from here. The FBI invited the Iowa DCI to couple, prior to storming a Nebraska farm which lay between Carter Lake and Eppley Airfield, an area already contentious with border disputes."

"Are you insinuating kids were literally restrained with shackles and chains, Rocco?"

Just then it hits me: the subtle irony and fine line between two consenting adults at play with sensory paraphernalia, and coerced confinement for the purpose of forced sex. The missing factor -- free will. Dah, I'm always the last to know.

"No, Maria, so much for hyperbole, though bondage ropes and trappings were identified in the raid. Seems that an elite alliance of wealthy men set out to assemble and coral a troupe of affluent young fellas -- healthy, innocent, sheltered kids from good homes. They were the targets. Our interrogation process netted details from a few of the alleged handlers. It appears the facility operated with a *concierge* service of sorts -- matching specific requests with specific conquests. Akin to customizing pedophiles with their victims."

"Imagine ordering up a tryst, like a Big Mac -- new meaning to: beef patty, sauce, pickle and buns." Fitting, yet very sad.

"You're not too far off, girl. Individuals were plainly pegged prior to kidnapping, based on their characteristics -- height, hair and eye color, build, ethnicity, and of course, age. The prey were roughly between five and fifteen years old. The *clients* were white-collar professionals, tycoons, moguls who were used to getting what they want and willing to pay for it."

"I can't even fathom the extent of the trade."

"Maria, check this out. . ."

CHAPTER 54

"...Think millionaires and billionaires who hailed from as far away as Burbank to the Bronx, from Minneapolis to Miami, all ultimately amassing in a podunk center situated on the fringes of Omaha. The cartel was quite pervasive and in existence for several years."

"That's lame. How could we not know about this before?"

"It was an elaborate underground business, Maria, totally decked out, no expense was spared. Designer fabrics, furnishings with an edgy contemporary style; crap, the electronics were state-of-the-art."

"Perchance," I mention, "the tech gear might also have served for entertaining, you know -- playing and recording videos."

"Bingo. In addition, each guest was given a topnotch recorded copy of his *interlude* as a memento."

"Christ, I need a shower after that note."

"Very likely the boys were slipped pills with or without their knowledge. We exposed a stash of high-end recreational dope -- GHB, X, Coke, mollies, anything you could snort or blow. And, of course, alcohol was abundant too, along with fentanyl patches."

"Fentanyl, isn't that a narcotic pain reliever? That med was prescribed to Grampie following lymphoma cancer surgery."

"Damn straight. It was originally in a slow-release form for chronic pain management, but, addicts and club-goers extract the opioid to experience a quick high 100 times more potent than morphine. Actually 'dance fever' and 'Tango' are a few of the street names -- rightfully so. Pretty dangerous shit, I hear."

"Okay," I nod, "now what are 'mollies'?"

"Oh, it's slang for amphetamines -- *speed*. Makes you restless, chatty. It's pretty similar to Ecstasy with a higher level of purity. Better living through chemistry."

"Man, you know your medicinals." As he continues his flash course, I sit puzzled, wondering if Chip has ever dabbled. "Please keep this shit out of our schools and our kids' hands."

"Doin' my best, ma'am."

"So Rocco, back to the fancy fantasy farm. I'm imagining an upscale whore house with all the goodies, except, dudes only."

"That's about right. A brothel -- without pussy."

I peek around, uneasy with Chip in earshot. My suspicion flares. "And who, pray tell, were the go-betweens, brokering the illicit exchanges? The body snatchers?"

"Maria, the big picture is mind-blowing."

Yet before I can brace for the news, Rocco steps out to take a call, about the same time Chip steams in.

"Mom, we need to talk." He fidgets, paces, joins me on the bench. Lily's got me freaking nuts. I can't think of anything else."

"Why so?" I study his eyes, "Tell me about it."

"Do you know the group, Maroon 5?"

He doesn't wait for a reply. "They sing this song, "One More Night," and it nails me."

"How so, honey?"

"The record tells how this girl makes a guy so crazy he stops using his head. How her lipstick gets him so out of breath. He can't control his feelings for her. That's me! I feel like a moron. Even though I respect Lily, when I see her I get butterflies in my gut and I wanna jump her -- all the time. I'm obsessed."

Uh huh, I think, I know how the love muscle works. "Sweetie, remember that you're older, more experienced than Lily, and she's fragile now. Didn't you feel the same way about Nataliya, in the beginning?"

"No, never; I swear. Nataliya has beauty and brains, but *gets* me."

"Young love is precious, Chip. Slow down, take baby steps. Don't screw it up by rushing ahead when she might not be ready. You can probably have it all; just not all at once."

Not certain my advice was helpful; then again, it's difficult fulfilling both roles of mother and father to a teenager.

CHAPTER 55

Chip blasts back to his room when Rocco returns.

"Here's the thing, Maria," Rocco confides, "our initial findings steered us to Headmaster Shelton at Immaculate Mary when we arrested him for videotaping fellas in the john. Little did we know he was assisting the pedophile ring by profiling."

"You mean he photographed kids so the rich folk could *pre-select* their choices?"

"Exacatackly. Also, we underestimated the size of the enterprise," shaking his head and pursing his lips, "until recently when we uncovered filming equipment in bathrooms at two other suburban schools."

"Oh my, are they Catholic too?" I hold my breath, mindful that another scandal is the last thing my Church needs.

"No, no -- the dickwads are equal opportunity offenders; they assault all denominations. Seriously, a few *pervs* even requested an NJB -- *nice Jewish boy* -- because they'd been circumcised."

"Creepy. Some predators must prefer to be PC when it comes to rape. *Mazel tov* in nailing those bastards to the cross."

"Hopefully we've got more than just luck on our side and that the indictments will stick. It's finally coming together."

"Let me get this straight: the drugs, Joey Gannon's disappearance, Shelton and the other school deans -- all meshed for a seamless inter-state conspiracy?"

"You got it. Actually the booming business included children from about nine states: Illinois, Indiana, Kansas, Missouri, Minnesota, Wisconsin and Michigan. That's along with Iowa and Nebraska. Right now we're reexamining earlier kidnappings, disappearances, and runaways, with the possibility that some of those youngsters might have been snapped up by the organization. We're reviewing all cases, open and closed; also custody battles where we originally believed one parent absconded with an offspring."

Rocco peels away.

* * *

I take a minute to digest the past events. From the boys' abductions, to their enslavement, to their rescue -- the fear, the horror, the reality. I collapse down.

I close my eyes and lament: how can my God allow man to be so cruel?

CHAPTER 56

I welcome the new day sun with a new attitude. One monthly magazine I subscribe to recommends that women warrant a good cry once a week -- men, about once a month. Hormones, the weather, relationships, hell, simply existing, take a toll on homo sapiens. Crying apparently relieves stress, elevates your mood, and can actually release pent-up feelings.

I reconsider and forgive the Lord for His stance on *not* interfering with our choices -- regardless of how rotten. Big of me, huh? Yes, I relish my freedom of choice, just not everyone's -- like the human demons who walk the earth deploying neither decency nor discretion.

I wish for Lily to be harbored from harm; I yearn for Joey Gannon, all young alter boys, and every child to be protected from perverts and priests, and/or perv priests. I pine for Chip's eternal safety. I flashback to a movie clip from *Crash* where the locksmith's daughter dons an invisible cloak, shielding her from all danger and stray bullets. Where are *our* cloaks?

In grade school Catechism we learned that St. Michael defended God's army against Lucifer, leader of the rebellious fallen angels. I guess he didn't win.

* * *

I unplug the charged cell, amplify the volume and commence sorting through overnight posts. Friend, Emma left a voicemail around midnight: *Maria, reserved a bed & breakfast spot for us near Dubuque next weekend. Remember: Eat, drink, and be merry, for tomorrow we may diet! Thoughts?*

A girls' weekend away brings to mind over-indulging in food and spirits. Perfect. I begin texting her back, promising to give her a jingle later, when a call chimes in from Clancy.

"Good morning." I smile as I scurry downstairs toward the kitchen to brew coffee.

"Hey, babe, what ya doin'?"

"Thinking of you." Truth is, my mouth waters and my peek-a-boo parts pulse when I envision the sparks from Clancy's tongue deep within...

"Nice, I could doze five or six hours, swing by your place, and you could show me what's on your mind."

"Alrighty then, Ace." The guy is a horndog, but then again I feel up to the challenge. "Around noon?" Figure Chip will have bounced by then and I can finish up paperwork for the condo, and confirm details with Emma.

"Sure. Should I pick up lunch on the way?"

"Nah, we'll find something here to munch."

CHAPTER 57

"Maria, I'm pumped for our pajama party Friday. Hope you've saved some secrets for me -- ones you haven't shared with anyone else."

"*Fait accompli.* Done deal, Emma. Besides, nobody is fascinated with my dysfunctional bio quite like you."

The missy is a Chatty Cathy -- referring to a throwback doll from the '60s, who repeated random phrases incessantly when a pull cord was tugged. At school, we nicknamed my mate, *DD*, for *The Des*

Moines Dispatch, our local daily rag. If the girl didn't know it, it fucking never happened!

"Sista, I want the facts and all the intimate details. Especially when it comes to your hose jockey Clancy, and the blather concerning our *dear* friend, Frankie."

Emma loves to dish the dirt, and my life is fodder for her. She has nursed me through a nasty break-up with Frankie, the summer before college, when I reeked of innocence. Consequently, her concern for him is less than genuine. Between us, gossip girl knows where all the bones are buried.

"Hey, I'm on it. It's likely something may happen today with fire boy, so I need to scoot. See you soon; love ya."

I cut off and dial up Jason, regarding renovation progress on the bungalow. I picture his rock-hard... *abs*, before glancing down to bullet-points on my hit list. We exchange greetings, discuss final figures and the completion date, concluding our business in about twenty minutes. I'm eager to prepare for Clancy's visit.

* * *

I'm struck with a plan to play pretend and dress-up in my high school cheerleading duds, kind of a nostalgia vibe. After all, it hasn't been *that* many years since I led the squad. The outfit does seem shorter though, tighter -- possibly a bit constricted in the butt and bust too. Even so, I reckon if I suit up *sans panties*, Clancy won't focus the snug fit in the derriere. And billowing breasts -- well, what's to talk about? By no means do guys turn down those succulent puppies.

I wind my honey-blond tousled tresses into a ponytail; the taut facial skin produces a bonus -- an unwrinkled porcelain surface, almost a mini face-lift. Choose to brave the light of day by shunning make-up and instead, crimp eyelashes prior to smearing on charcoal mascara, then dab grapefruit gloss across my lips before smacking together.

Quickly I slather peppermint sole-mate over tootsies, ahead of touching up a two-week-old pedicure. Never certain what your man might be into -- like toe nibbling.

I'm reminded of the intensity of date prep. My friends with daughters typically discuss the time and expense associated with *grooming*. From salon appointments for highlights or lowlights, to designer cuts and curls. From hair removal, such as eyebrow-threading, upper-lip tweezing, or Brazilian waxing, to hair extensions, weaves, and wigs. Beauty treatments for fingernails, including trimming, filing, moisturizing, polishing, applying acrylics, decals and gems, to attending all cuticles -- hence the term, mani-pedi.

Wow, now add: cosmetics, wardrobe, jewelry, accessories (including tats and piercings), fragrance, capped white teeth, a nose job, a boob job, and body sculpting with either a personal trainer or plastic surgeon. The sheer scheduling and servicing of the female anatomy -- staggering. Needless to say, quite an investment too.

Question: Are we that *beautiful,* or that *ugly?*

Vanity, thy name is woman.

CHAPTER 58

I greet Clancy at the front door with a rush of uncertainty. Fortunately he displays leering eyes partnered with a devil's grin. Then, upon further inspection, his fickle fingers fly beneath my skirt for an examination. He has always claimed to be a doctor, specializing in Oral Gynecology. As I ingest his husky aroma, he discovers my secret and screeches, "Eureka!" His expression is attributed to Archimedes -- a sudden, unexpected realization. Translation: *I found it!*

Most definitely he did. And then, again.

* * *

"Dude," I tease, "we didn't even make it to the bedroom." I snicker as I pick myself up from the entry bench and rustle my pleated crumpled skirt back into place.

"You know Maria, I've never been credited with a plethora of patience, especially when it comes to sexual pursuits." He shrugs his shoulders and presents a palms up pose. "Guilty as charged."

"I wasn't accusing you, babe. Takes two to tango; and indeed we did cut a rug."

"Yep. Most times I'm cool just living in the moment. We're over twenty-one and consensual. And, we're alone." Clancy shoots a look-see both directions surveying the house. "Right?"

"Yes, dear. Chip is gone and not due back for hours."

"Hot damn! What say we snatch a quick snack and head to your room where you can serenade me with school spirit. On second thought, forget lunch." He sails upstairs.

I nod affably. A girl deserves an orgasm whenever possible -- gots to enjoy the goods between dry spells. At once I begin rehearsing a cheer from days gone by with the stands full of football fans:

Be aggressive

B-E aggressive!

B-E-A-G-G-R-E-S-S-I-V-E

Be aggressive!

"Be there in a minute, Clancy," I holler, "gonna set my cell on vibrate first." Hmm, *vibrate* gives me a thought.

I hasten to the kitchen counter to behold a voicemail from brother Nick regarding his invite for Chip and me for dinner tonight. I begin texting our RSVP when I'm interrupted with a new message from Rocco: *"Maria, 911!"*

CHAPTER 59

I swallow hard and press #4, speed-dialing Rocco.

"Maria, bad news, we've picked up Chip with a number of his classmates -- for prescription drug possession. He's being held at the Polk County Juvenile Center on East 12ᵗʰ until he can be processed."

"Sonofabitch!" If I were a guy, I would immediately go limp. Rather, for a few seconds, I freeze like a statue. "Seriously, boss, this is no April Fool's gag?"

"Girl, it's September; and no, it's no joke. But it isn't life or death either, just a wake-up call. Good thing he's under eighteen. If you want, I'll hang here awhile. How long do you think you'll be?"

Shit, I remember Mom always saying she felt the most unsettled when life seemed to be going well -- waiting for the other proverbial shoe to drop. Sure enough, a stampede.

"I'll shoot your way shortly, Rocco. Thanks."

After looking around nervously, with alarms sounding in my head, I plunk down on a kitchen stool with a thud. I cross myself, then gasp a few deep cleansing breaths.

"*Maria!*" croons Clancy from upstairs. "Something here I want you to see."

Terrifimundo. Now it's time to share the glorious news of my son, with my naked lover tucked snug like a bug in my bed. Undoubtedly this will kill the switch on today's affair and possibly future escapades.

Suitors, like Clancy, are a different breed, having dodged the marital trail a time or two. Many are either unwilling or unfamiliar with sacrifice for the greater good. As a child I learned: *Love begins when you put someone else's needs ahead of your own.* That said, would Clancy ever be onboard with the burden of responsibility required by the parent trap? Who am I to burst his duty-free bubble?

Surprisingly, Clancy does not deal with our coital interruption with disdain. Instead he displays kindness and understanding. Perhaps his heart is at odds with his head -- one of his heads anyway. Regardless, he presses his lips on mine before parting. A good sign.

* * *

When I arrive at the detention center, anxiety engulfs me. This sucks. Especially showing up here alone -- without a spouse or partner. It's tough trying to balance both the grace and grit needed to discipline a young man.

What signs have I missed? I picture the pills in my bathroom medicine cabinet. Tablets I've been prescribed: a muscle relaxant for a pinched nerve; a sleep remedy after Michael's death; an anti-inflammatory for an injured knee; an antibiotic for strep throat. Nothing very exotic, though possibly party favs. I'm not young and dumb anymore, though I can't speak for the millennials, or Generation X, Y or whatever. All said, what is the attraction to drugs? To fit in? To rebel? To experiment? To get high and forget the world?

I consider lingo from the Top 40 playlist -- FUN: *my friends are in the bathroom getting higher than the Empire State*; Ed Sheeran: *white lips, paleface, breathing in snowflakes, burnt lungs, sour taste*; and Lorde: *trippin' in the bathroom, bloodstains, ball gowns, trashin' the hotel room, we crave a different kind of buzz.* Yes, they do. And, One Republic's release, *"Everything that kills me, makes me feel alive."*

"Hey there," Rocco bellows. As he inches closer, he confides, "You look a little *worn*, Maria."

"Ya think?" I try to downplay his comment, but of course I know an hour earlier I had worn Clancy like a tattoo all over my body. I deliberate if Rocco is referring to my legitimate mental anguish over Chip's mess-up, or my carnal cardio workout?

They say that men can *smell* sex on a woman. Oh, joy! Just what I want from my kissin' cousin.

CHAPTER 60

"Really, Rocco? Chip has been abusing prescription meds? I don't buy it. There's nothing you can say to convince me." My heart hammers in time with my pounding head.

'Maria, you're not alone. Most moms and dads are in denial about their kids' drug involvement."

"Dude, here's the thing. When Chip was twelve, his partner from tennis camp shoplifted a CD from K-Mart. A few years later, some of his school buddies pinched a sack of recycled cans from a Git-'n-Gone storage bin, to collect the deposit refund. 'Tell me with whom you go, and I'll tell you what you are,' Nonnie says. Lesson learned: get new friends -- he did! But now, Chip stealing and misusing drugs? Uh, uh. I know my kid. He's not a thief. He's not an addict."

"Cuz, the sheer ignorance of parents places them in a position of passive pushers -- by not securing or disposing of unused medications. Mind your meds. If a kid can swallow it, smoke it, inhale it, or inject it -- they want it. It's far easier for adolescents nowadays to get hold of narcotics, than say, beer or marijuana. Immediate family members are also clueless as to the widespread severity of the problem. Engagement is a basic component of reducing the risk of substance abuse."

"Rocco, I'm engaged. Hear me out. Yes, he's the pinball king -- most days rolling between mania and depression. And, he's impulsive with a scattered thought process; rightfully so, he's a teenager. But man, this goes way beyond." I shoot a side-glance toward him, when his face creases into a grin.

"Okay Maria, Chip is working for us. No, he's not a drug lord or a crook."

"Fucker! I knew it. You are *evil.*" My shoulders slump as I blow a sigh of relief, though at the same time I ache for the folks in front of me, filing in to collect their delinquents.

Recently I penned a letter to the editor of the *Des Moines Dispatch* with my concerns charging juveniles as adults in some crimes. Ludicrous! Surely by virtue of minor age, diminished competency, and delayed maturity, teens are not yet programmed to *get it.* I'm not allowed to change my birthdate to collect Social Security early, so why do judges force juveniles to change their age in order to prosecute in adult criminal court?

* * *

Once Chip and I are united, Rocco steers us into a small alcove flanking the interrogation room, to thank Chip personally on behalf of the force for his undercover service. I'm taken aback when I realize he smeared his own reputation; his classmates will never know he was innocent of the charges, and only participated as a pawn for the sting operation. I'm in awe and very proud of my son.

"Chip, you crushed it. Great job." I snake my arm around his neck and pull him in for a cheek smooch. "Boy, why do you do this? Attention? Friendship? Boredom?"

His eyes search the sky. "Pretty much, FOMO."

"Huh? What the hell is that?"

"Fear of missing out."

"And, that means what to me?"

"Mom, when I'm working with Rocco and the PD, I get to be part of the fast crowd -- make bad choices, without the consequences. Dave Matthews says: 'sometimes it's better to be somebody else.' I get to be an idiot, instead of a goody all the time. Kids don't know I'm a snitch, so they accept me -- it's the best of both worlds. I'm thinking about police work or maybe the FBI for a career."

Christ, what have I done? My own *Danger Ranger.*

CHAPTER 61

I was anticipating the weekend ahead, chillin' with Emma in Dubuque, but first things first -- dinner for us tonight with brother Nick and Gina. Without a doubt, Chip will be stoked after his involvement with the school drug syndicate, but that subject is off-limits for public ears. Perhaps we can steer the meal prattle toward politics or religion -- touchy topics for most table-mates, but safer than today's reenactment.

* * *

"Chip, let's do this," I holler from the bottom of the stairs. "We need to skedaddle." I yank the fridge open and extract a bottle of a newly-released sparkling nectar, XXIV KARAT, with actual flecks of floating glittering gold. I pop the California Grand Cuvee into a black-and-white striped bag for Gina, the hostess with the mostess. I remember the well-known dictum: guests should always arrive bearing gifts.

We pull up the meandering driveway to a regal sprawling brick ranch, just as Nick is changing a light bulb at the front door. We park in front of his five-car garage and I spy equipment for home building -- a tractor with a backhoe, a ditch witch, and the usual suspects for surviving Iowa summers and winters -- a John Deere riding mower and snow blower. Also visible are their private vehicles -- a Mars Red Mercedes Convertible and the workhorse, a GMC Onyx Black Sierra.

My bro greets us with a genuine smile while we share an air-kiss and a pat on the back for Chip. "Hey, kiddo, how's it feel to finally be a senior? And, how's the college search progressing?"

"No pressure yet, I'm all over it Uncle Nick. Here, this is for Aunt Gina," as he hands over the wine sack.

We scuttle inside. Chip plops himself in front of the TV which is broadcasting the second half of a World Cup qualifier: USA vs. Mexico. After embracing my sister-in-law, I'm passed a flute of Cabernet Sauvignon from Sonoma County 2009. After a swig and of the vino, I identify a ripe flavor of black cherry, spice and currants. Without a doubt we will be dining on either beef or pasta. M'mm, m'mm good!

"Maria, Nicky tells me you're finishing up your remodel. What's next on the agenda?" She stands at the stove in front of a stock pot with a large slotted spoon, straining and lifting out homemade gnocchi -- petite potato pillows -- onto a platter. *My* recipe consists of ricotta cheese, in place of the potato base, for a lighter fare and because my grandmother hails from Northern Italy while Gina's was born in Sicily. They kind of do things back-assward down south. Either way, the time-consuming delicacy is a delight after smothering in a marinara sauce with grated Romano. "Would you pull things together for the salad?"

"Sure." I dump a package of mixed greens into a brightly-colored over-sized round bowl, hand-painted by her mom. As I sprinkle on seasoned salt, pepper, crushed sweet basil, olive, oil and balsamic vinegar, I look at Gina and resume. "I'm considering trying my hand at a speck house next. What do ya think?" I complete my task by adding fresh finely-shredded Parmesan.

"Sounds speculative. If it doesn't sell right away, are you prepared to move in? This is our twelfth home in as many years. Nowadays I don't even unpack seasonal stuff -- Easter, Halloween, Christmas, until we need it. We settle in, stage our furniture and belongings, and pretty much sell to the highest bidder. Twice, Nicky sold our homes to custom clients scheduled for their first appointment. Once, he even sold our home with all the furnishings! It gets old, but it provides us with a great income."

"God knows, he has a stellar reputation. He works hard and gives his customers what *they* want."

Granted, he's sharp, the smartest thing he ever did however, was marry Gina. I miss that -- having a best friend and lover to boot.

Nick charges into the kitchen with a grim look on his face. "Hey Maria, is your phone off?" I knew I'd flipped it to *silent* for a little peace. "Rocco's been trying to reach you. Here." He hands his cell to me.

"Girl, it's go-time!"

CHAPTER 62

"Hey, I'll call you back from my cell." I return Nick's phone to him, excuse myself and hightail out of the kitchen onto a three-season porch. I crouch by the corner window for better reception.

"Maria, wanted you and Chip to rally here at the house to finalize our covert affairs. Sounds like you're dining at your bro's tonight. Can you shoot by the palace after?"

"Definitely." I know he's referring to the police station for our rendezvous point, but I thought our reconnaissance had already concluded, so my mind is a little muddled. "How 'bout some details, bucko? Is this urgent?" His cryptic message leaves me perplexed.

"Negatory. Just wanted to guarantee we talked. My bad. Sometimes I forget you're a civilian. You're not expected to be available 24/7."

"Gotcha. When we wrap up here, we'll bounce. In about an hour."

We sit down to eat, but first recite Grace Before Meals: *Bless us, O Lord, and these Thy gifts, which we are about to receive from Thy bounty, through Christ our Lord. Amen.*

Then Nick takes the lead at table talk. "Funny story. When Gina and I invited Nonnie for brunch a few weeks ago, I picked some flowers for her from our garden. Immediately I started wheezing and sneezing. "Nonnie, please excuse me, I have to take an *Allegra*."

"Oh honey, I'm sorry, I didn't know you had *that* problem."

"She cupped a hand over her mouth, cringing in embarrassment. I laughed my ass off and said, 'No, Nonnie, I don't. But, if I did, you would be the absolute last person I'd tell'!"

We chuckle, though Chip rotates his eyes, most likely thinking the tale is trite. He proceeds to share his intentions to pursue a few courses in Criminal Justice after graduation next summer. He could collect credit hours from DMACC, a community college in Ankeny, and at the same time check out the requirements for the AA Degree.

Nick and I kibitz about homebuilding: housing starts, existing inventory, and the Federal Reserve Bank's Beige Book findings, which forecast interest rates, and ultimately future home sales.

As we leap up to leave, Gina asks, "Chip, please email us a copy of your soccer schedule. We'd love to come see a game or two."

We exclaim, "Ciao," before blazing away. Next stop: the Des Moines Police Department.

* * *

I had just parked the Beamer, when a voice echoes.

"Maria, over here." Chip and I spin around and witness Rocco perched atop a fire hydrant, puffing drags from a cigarette.

"Mister, since when did you start smoking?" Indeed I'm not aware of everything in his life, but I've never seen the guy with a cancer stick before.

"Hey there. It's not what you think, Maria. It's an e-cigarette." He waves the flameless battery-operated device in the air. "No tobacco, no tar and carcinogens."

"Right, just a steady stream of liquid nicotine -- cuz that's *so* healthy. Why, Rocco? You're better than that." Straightaway I regret my comments. *Remember: don't judge.*

"I've been under a lot of stress, and I'm trying to control anxiety. I'm restricted from addictive meds, Xanax or Valium. And *this*," he flips his wrist, "is legal."

Chip draws closer, trains his sites on Rocco and insists, "Man, whatever gets you through the night."

I feel like crap. I turn to apologize to my cousin when Det. Wittry sprints out to us.

"Rocco, we just got word -- your wife's been *kidnapped!*"

CHAPTER 63

Rocco torpedoes up, bellowing fury and begins shaking his partner. "Ryne, where's Eden?" If he wasn't unglued before, this turn of events will surely put him over the edge. "Fucking shit, who's at the bottom of this?"

"Man, calm down. We got a GPS tracer from the call. It's a warehouse off Euclid and Seventh in East Village. SWAT Team has already been deployed and is in position."

"Ryne, who's got my wife? And why?" He begs for frightening clarity.

Holy buckets. Chip and I drill eyes on each other, figuring we should scram. "We're gonna split and let you get going. Stay strong, Rocco." I put a hand out, catch his sleeve cuff and squeeze.

We storm toward our car, I slide in behind the wheel. "Chip, I'll drop you off at home and then I'm heading to the scene." I feel a tad conflicted with my decision to join up without an invite, though I refuse to be left out.

"No way, Mom. You know I heard the address too; I'll be right behind you."

Point taken. I pinch my lips together, then bite on them. I presume if I say *no*, Chip will ratchet up the pressure and possibly defy me anyway -- like I would. So, I cave. "Ok, but promise you'll stay in the car."

* * *

We bolt to the scene. It resembles Christmas with red, white, yellow and blue blinking lights aglow -- except for the scores of fire trucks and EMTs in evidence. Below a steep, muddy slope adjacent to the hostage hideaway, stands a troop of heavily-armed officers suited in body armor, lugging ballistic shields. Also in startling view is the arsenal: assault and sniper rifles, breaching shotguns, flash grenades and concussion bombs -- all poised for a rescue -- or a bloody revolt.

"Chip, stay here!" I bark. I wag my index pointer toward him for added impact.

My gaze scans the hillside incessantly, darting to Rocco situated next to the captain. I'm afraid my curiosity gives way to caution when I straggle in their direction. But before I can reach them, I hear, *Pop!*

I lunge to the ground. It sounded like someone crunched a shot, though I can't decipher from my position where the sound originated. I crawl toward an ambulance, reasoning it might be out of range. All I need is bullets licking at my feet! I haul up, seeking safety.

"Hey," I call out to the bus driver, "my cousin is being held over there," I direct a finger toward the structure. "Any word?"

"Sorry, ma'am, we aren't privy to that info. The guy with the headphones, over there," (he aims his attention toward Captain Baxter) "is in charge of the operation."

"What was that *bang* I heard?"

"Can't say, but I'm told the warehouse is a distribution center for fertilizer, so you want to be careful. If that stuff combusts -- we're all goin' to the moon."

"Good to know."

BOOM!!

CHAPTER 64

The ground rumbles, then an explosion rocks the earth. As my eyes adjust and become accustomed to my surroundings, I realize I've been tossed through the air fifteen feet, landing on my booty -- plenty of padding there. Before me blazes a fireball the size of the Des Moines Capitol. I sniff, inhaling a stinging abrasive gas, causing tears to flood my face. The stink sticks to my skin and hangs in my hair. Immediately I sense a nauseous stomach along with a piercing headache. Can it be *fertilizer?*

Gradually I raise myself up and in slo-mo, race through the hazy atmosphere toward Rocco. He stands alone, hands crossed over each other. He speaks first. "Maria, she's gonna be okay! Eden is gonna be okay; and so is the baby."

"What *baby?*" I repeat in bewilderment.

"She's pregnant, eight weeks pregnant." He swipes a fist across his mouth nervously, then lets out a big sigh.

"Christ! Why didn't you tell us earlier, Rocco?"

"Because Eden is old school. Her mom told her not to share the news until she had passed the first trimester. I just do what I'm told."

No doubt -- history verifies that he's perused the wedding aisle a few too many times previously. "Of course. I understand nowadays about one in four women miscarry. Maybe it's something in the water." For the first time I perceive a faint smile from my cousin. "But, what the hell is this all about cuz?" I twist toward a trail of destruction, turning my palms up in ambivalence.

Before he can respond, the Captain approaches and Rocco rotates over to him. Out of the corner of my view, I spot Chip, so I schlep his way.

"What the fuck?" I spew. "What does, *'stay here'* mean to you?"

"Well, Mom, I am *here*. Seriously, sometimes you get so petty over a word or two." He shrugs his shoulders, genuinely unaware that he has defied me.

"Really? And you're how old now?" I'm annoyed, though mindful that the analogy is lost in translation. "This is treacherous territory, honey. This crap we're breathing could be frying our lungs as we speak." I gasp to take in a breath, then sputter. "We need to bail. Stay with me!"

CHAPTER 65

As we amble toward the Beamer, I ogle a squatty square storage hut on the outer perimeter of the premises. My intuition impels me to explore further. I'm hoping the hovel houses fresh air and not the stench of fertilizer -- or a latrine for that matter. I pluck at a rusty lever and wrench open the grizzled door. "Chip, step back," I caution. "I don't know what we might find." Honestly I figure we could run across a rat, or snake, or some other repulsive critter.

"Holy shit!" Lo and behold on the dirt floor, surrounded by water pumps and pipes, lay my grade school chum, Lynn Bea. Her hands and legs are bound behind her back with nylon line, and a grungy cloth is rammed in her jaw. Pure terror ricochets in her eyes as they jet back and forth.

I rush to remove the mouth muzzle when Chip screams, "Mom!"

I turn toward him, stunned to see he has a revolver pressed against his temple. Holding the piece is Jack Crew, the high school soccer coach. "Please!" I shriek. "Let my son go! Take me instead." I've already lost a husband, I'll be damned if anyone is taking my kid.

I fly up and fling my arms in surrender mode. I recognize the perp's sidearm -- a Beretta M9, probably a service pistol from either Iraq or Afghanistan. Lynn had been stationed in the Middle East with the National Guard a few years ago. Had she and Crew possibly crossed paths there?

"You two get to the ground," growls our captor, wildly wielding his weapon. "You think you're all so fucking smart, revealing our racket at school. But lady, what you failed to focus on is the endless, frantic, compulsion of sexual addiction. You think I like being dictated by my *dick?*"

As we scuttle down, I consider whether Crew's erratic behavior stems from drug use or a voracious appetite for degenerate deeds. Whatever, the creep makes my skin crawl. Unlikely I will muster much pity for the fool, though I will hear him out.

"I'm sorry, Coach," I begin, "but you did bring on your own grief with your risky choices." Pretty cheeky, I think.

"Maybe so. I remember when seedy magazines, porn sites and male strippers were enough to get me off."

He wants to talk, which could maybe buy us some time, so I reel him in. "Sure, I get that."

"But the stress, anxiety, and depression caught up with me and I began using narcotics. Eventually my impulses progressed and I tailored my attacks to young boys for gratification. I'm not proud."

Clearly the guy is overcome with remorse -- tears stream as he rubs his face. Gradually I stand while continuing to talk, "The studies I've seen claim that shame is at the heart of philandering. Does that make sense?"

As he chews his lip and his gazes drifts upward, abruptly I tap Chip's leg with my foot, then grope for Crew's gun.

CHAPTER 66

Chip jerks Crew's ankle, causing his legs to buckle, while I fumble for his firearm.

"Honey, cut Lynn loose, then use the cord to tie up the coach," I order my son.

"Please, please don't turn me in," Crew pleads with his fingers clutched in a prayer position. "I've heard inmates are heartless with child molesters."

"Shucks. Probably should have considered that earlier, dude."

Chip finishes fortifying the line around Crew's limbs as I comb my pockets for my cell to notify the nearby cavalry. But before I can connect, the door springs open and Rocco bursts in.

"Maria," cries Rocco, "stand-down. I'll take it from here."

Smart move; my hands are trembling. He gently pries the gun from my hands while promptly sizing up the situation. Next, with momentum and enthusiasm, he kicks Crew square in the nards. I feel sucker-punched just watching such a cruel act. Suddenly a familiar quote from either John Wayne or maybe George Jetson flashes across my right brain: *a man's gotta do what a man's gotta do.*

Crew cringes while exhaling expletives.

"Thanks, Rocco; I guess," I add.

He stoops lower, cuts the coach's bindings and restrains him with cuffs instead. "Is the girl hurt? Does she need a medic?"

"I'm good," Lynn mutters.

"I'll send for a bus anyway." He heaves his prisoner up and drags him outside as he mirandizes him.

"Mom, if you guys are okay, I'm gonna step out to make a few calls," Chip says.

"Swell. Don't stray far off though."

I bend and help lift my friend into a sitting position. I brush her brown bangs out of her black-olive eyes and cradle her head. "Seriously, are you alright?" Her nose is bleeding, her lip is lanced and her previously-white designer tee is tattered and torn.

"Damn, Maria, quit fussing. I'm made from the same tough Italian stuff as you."

"That goes without saying. But now, tell me, how the hell did you wind up here?"

"Well, I met Jack in Iraq; we were both with the Guard. I wasn't aware of his tendency toward young boys back then. We hung out, chummed around because we were both from Des Moines. I left when my stint was over, and he stayed behind for another year."

"Sure," I nod.

"I got a text two days ago. He wanted to meet for lunch at Chux, the pizzeria in uptown Lowland Park. When I showed up he hustled me into his car and we blazed away. I got a little twinge in my tummy, and alarms went off in my head...

"Unfortunately, I snubbed the signs."

CHAPTER 67

We rally with Rocco at the station to give statements, then Chip and I sign our affidavits.

Next, Lynn has her say: "Coach Crew and I had blasted away a few blocks, when we met up with a couple of rogue thugs driving in a late-model Durango. Admittedly I was apprehensive and soon scared shitless when I was overpowered, transferred to the SUV, and smothered with a smelly scarf. I don't remember anything after that until I came to this morning in the hut."

"You're a tough cookie, Lynn," Rocco boasts. "Evidently Crew and his brutes kept you sedated so they could empty out your bank accounts, ransack your home, and ready themselves for a getaway to an off-shore destination."

I peek over toward my pal and notice she's in *freak mode.*

"What? Why me?"

"I'm gonna assume you shared personal info while you and the guy were serving out country. After all, it's common knowledge you oversee a sizeable hedge fund with a local wealth management firm. Don't fret," Rocco adds, "we've recovered all the assets, cash and your valuables."

"So the scumbags were fleeing the country. Hoping to set up another sleazy sex ring somewhere else?"

"Apparently so, Maria -- probably in Bermuda or perhaps in the Caribbean, maybe Jamaica. To their dismay though, we've collected enough evidence to send the bastards up state for years to come."

"Bam!" Chip cries. "Got their comeuppance."

* * *

We three cram into the convertible and careen toward home.

"Hey, Maria," Lynn coaxes, "do you recall the prank we pulled in fourth grade -- Miss Newgent's class?"

"Uh, pretty hard to forget. We spent four Saturdays in a row starching and ironing the nuns' habits for punishment."

Chip perks up and repeats, *"Punishment?* Now you got my attention. What'd ya girls do -- set fire to the school?"

"Nah, nothing that bold," Lynn chuckles. "But who'd a thunk our fannies would get flagged for adding food coloring to the holy water fonts?"

"Personally I relished the purple tint -- it complemented the priests' Lenten vestments. I'm convinced our only real mistake was in tinting *all* the fountains, including the baptismal well."

"Yeah, but it was a nice touch. And the lavender fingerprints on Sister Mary Gabriel's wimple was a stitch."

"Is that the white cardboard bib the sisters wore?"

"No, no; that's a guimpe. Member?"

"Oh hell, all those years of religious education and now my mind's gone to Cleveland."

"You know, Maria, we've had some good times, broke a few rules along the way. That said, we're still *good girls.* One day, years from now, when we reach the pearly gates, St. Peter's gonna pass us right on through."

And I think, yes, dear sweet Lynn, *you* will certainly skate straight to Heaven. But me -- well, I'm *not* blushing.

CPSIA information can be obtained at www.ICGtesting.com
Printed in the USA
LVOW11s2039100116

469539LV00002B/7/P